Amalie Berlin lives with her family and her critters in Southern Ohio, and writes quirky and independent characters for Mills & Boon Medical Romance. She likes to buck expectations with unusual settings and situations, and believes humour can be used powerfully to illuminate the truth—especially when juxtaposed against intense emotions. Love is stronger and more satisfying when your partner can make you laugh through the times when you don't have the luxury of tears.

REUNITED IN THE SNOW

AMALIE BERLIN

MILLS & BOON

Published in Great Britain 2019
by Mills & Boon, an imprint of HarperCollins*Publishers*
1 London Bridge Street, London, SE1 9GF

© 2019 Amalie Berlin

ISBN: 978-0-263-08093-3

MIX
Paper from
responsible sources
FSC® C007454

This book is produced from independently certified FSC™ paper
to ensure responsible forest management.
For more information visit www.harpercollins.co.uk/green.

Printed and bound in Great Britain
by CPI Group (UK) Ltd, Croydon, CR0 4YY

Northamptonshire
Libraries

E

To my Mamaw Mary, who reads more than any other person I ever met—because she's awesome—and who still reads all of my books. Except for the sexy parts. (I don't know if that's true but I want to believe it, so I do, no matter what anyone else says. La-la-la-la, I can't hear you!)

CHAPTER ONE

DR. LIA MONTERROSA had not inherited the seafaring, adventurous spirit of her Portuguese ancestors. But she talked a good game.

None of her traveling companions appeared to be any more sprightly than she was after the long, arduous journey. Each lugged modest amounts of luggage down the pristine, shiny corridors of the brand-new Antarctic research station where they'd just arrived, no spring in any thick-booted step. All of them were carrying what would see them through the long months of a dark Antarctic winter.

She'd heard various reasons for coming—once-in-a-lifetime experience, work they wanted to do and could best accomplish locked up for eight solid months with fifty strangers. For her, that was the upside of her trip—being surrounded by people who didn't know her, and therefore had no expectations about how she should behave. She didn't have to be the strongest person on the planet, and she didn't have to be the most docile, polite one, either.

But her ex-fiancé was who she'd come to find. To ask why he was her ex. What had happened during the four days she'd been gone, home in Portugal, that had made him decide he didn't love her anymore, didn't want to marry her? To ask why he'd been cold enough to also go missing while she was filing paperwork with the Polícia Judiciária to locate her missing father.

He hadn't left a message. Hadn't scribbled his farewell on a sticky note affixed to the bathroom mirror. He'd just stopped answering her calls, and three days before her wedding, when she'd had a moment free to go back to London and look for him, as well, she'd found his flat vacated, job vacated, mobile phone canceled. He'd left her with the beautiful ring they'd painstakingly designed together, and a hole in her chest so big a truck could pass through.

But she would see him today, the end of too many months of torture. If fate was with her, he'd provide answers. Closure, if that was a real thing that actually happened, and not just some psychobabble placebo. Closure, no closure—it didn't really matter. The end was coming. The final end. The official end that had been denied her when she'd come home to find him gone.

Right on cue, her stomach plummeted—a sensation she should've become immune to by now, but which still had the ability to wrench away brief control of her extremities. Her booted foot scuffed the floor, but she didn't fall— walking was a little easier to recover from than errant hand-twitches in surgery when a slight wrong move could end a life. Knowing what had ended *them* would help, even if it was just another case of her not being enough. No matter how much she wanted to, she couldn't fix whatever she'd done wrong if she didn't know what it was.

"Dr. Monterrosa, you're in Pod C," her guide said, jerking her from her thousandth thought-spiral of this trip, and gesturing to a nondescript door with a circular window at head height—the kind peppering the station, and which reminded her of doors on boats.

The group all stopped long enough for the woman to add, "With you lot arriving at the end of summer, you're getting stacked where there is an open cabin."

And she was the only one in C, which would practically become a ghost town in little more than a week when she could probably have her pick of rooms. After Jordan and Zeke left. After West...

Lia opened her mouth to ask the number, but her fatigue was starting to show. The guide answered before she even formed the first sluggish word.

"Last door on the left, end of the hall."

With a soft, tired grunt, Lia hoisted one of her two meager bags onto her shoulder and entered without another word. Through the door and into a much dimmer hallway, somewhere obviously designed for sleeping through the twenty-four-hour days of summer.

She had about three seconds to see it as the door swung closed and the bright light from the corridor dissipated, but all she really saw was beige. Walls. Low-static carpeting. White doors dotting both sides of the hall. Snow blind, she waited only long enough for general shapes to form in her vision, allowing her to navigate without bumping into walls or running over strangers in the hallway.

Dr. Weston MacIntyre would never know what had hit him. She had the upper hand, and she needed it. He'd expect her to come at him with guns blazing, and that method had its own appeal. It might help her hide the hole and all the raw-hamburger emotions lining the inside.

Jordan knew she was coming. Her best friend from medical school and almost maid of honor had been the one to call Lia the day West had shown up at Fletcher Station, the person she'd gone to for help shutting down a wedding when hope was finally lost, but she hadn't even known if he was alive. She'd had months to prepare herself for this confrontation, to script every word and every motion in her head, compose the best emasculating zingers and lists of all the ways she would never, and had never, missed him. But with the starting gun ready to sound, the idea of actually saying any of those things left her cold. Colder than the balmy ten below that she'd walked through from the bus to the station. No one who went halfway around the world to find another person could honestly say she hadn't missed him. Hadn't worried. But it felt better to pretend. Lies could comfort.

She made a sharp right bend in the hallway and kept walking. Halfway to the end, her vision had cleared enough to see a tall, broad man with a black knit hat and an equally black beard standing outside the last two doors, keys in hand, staring in her direction.

In another couple of meters, her stomach did that dropping thing again and this time when her limb control faltered, the only thing that saved her from further humiliation was the meager stability offered by the suitcase rolling beside her.

West.

It was West.

Her polished, ever-immaculate fiancé. Former fiancé. But far scruffier.

Her whole world slowed down, and the remaining length of the hallway grew longer than the thousands of kilometers she'd traveled to reach this hallway with this man.

Instead of a tirade, her mind filled with all the times she'd walked toward him. Right back to that first time they'd met in a London hospital, when a newly minted general surgeon had required an assist and been told to pull one of the not-busy neurosurgical fellows. Her. And the way he'd watched her approaching after having her paged, down the hallway to where he loitered at the nurses' station, his eyes broadcasting bold, open interest until he'd heard her name. How she'd pretended not to notice the looks, how she'd managed to ignore her own attraction for three whole days before she'd asked *him* out.

London Lia did those things. London Lia was fearless.

At least on the outside. Because it was what everyone expected of her.

Lifting her chin, Lia held his gaze now, struggling to ignore the burst of other memories. All the church aisles they'd tried on looking for the perfect church for their wedding. When he'd looked at her with the promise of a long future dancing in his eyes, the future he delighted in planning and dreaming into existence with her.

Time sped back up. Her heart squeezed hard once, then began stomping a *chula* around her sternum, fast enough she'd have been silencing alarms on her fitness monitor if the battery hadn't died on the trip down. And her stomach, which had been lurching and freefalling for the duration of the trip, went hollow, and cold. Then the nausea hit.

He didn't speak or look away, just stared. There was an intensity in his gaze, but nothing loving. She'd call it a glare were it not for the pallor she could see when she got closer.

Was this it? The burning in her eyes said so. All happening before she'd even dropped off her luggage?

She wasn't ready.

What could she say? What had she even practiced? She was supposed to say something. She'd come all this way to say *things*. Learn things. Remove the weight of betrayal and loss that glittered on her left ring finger.

The ring that symbolized that future they'd planned weighted her finger and something like relief weighted her tongue. Relief. Regret. Betrayal.

If she'd slept at all on the way there, she would've been able to think. She'd be able to look away from his eyes, and her ears wouldn't be ringing in a way that made her worry about a stroke. She'd hear something other than her own loud, labored breathing in the dead space in her chest.

The Lia he knew would say the words. Slap him, maybe.

Shake answers out of him. *Something.* But whoever she was now didn't have that in her.

As the seconds stretched out his shock turned to something else, something harder, and she gave up the mental scramble for words to wait him out, watching anger flare in his eyes, bitterness turn the mouth she'd lived to kiss into a slash amid the facial hair she'd never before seen him wear.

But he didn't say anything, either. No words from either of them. The only acknowledgment that she had any more meaning to him than a stranger came in the form of gritted teeth.

As if he had any right to be angry with *her.* She hadn't left *him* practically at the altar.

She opened her mouth, but before she'd even mustered a word, he stepped past her and silently stormed down the hallway, rigid and straight. Angry. So angry, with her.

He was nearly to the bend, with his rigid posture and determination to yet again get away from her. She'd gone around the world to find him, but in that moment, she had no energy left to chase.

She closed her eyes and breathed slowly out.

In her memories, it seemed she was always walking toward him—down hallways, church aisles, even on staircases in the hospital where they'd meet for a quick kiss between patients or rounds. She didn't have it in her to watch him walking away. That was the only kindness afforded her by the manner of his leaving—she hadn't even seen it coming, let alone had to watch him going.

God, she was so stupid.

There were other Antarctic research stations she could've gone to. A whole world where no one knew her and she could sort herself out without pressure, get ready for the new life waiting for her outside of medicine. This wasn't going to be productive enough to endure the pain that went with it.

Bending her head, she pinched her eyes harder shut, so the pressure swirled colors and shadow to light behind her eyelids, blocking out the mental replay of things she'd obviously never have again with him.

And none of this should surprise her. Of course he didn't want to talk to her. She was the personification of the past, and West had always avoided talking about the past. Only the future. And she was no longer part of his future. Or she was only part of his immediate future, for the next ten days, until he could escape.

He would talk to her. She'd figure out what to say to him, what she really wanted to say, not just what her broken heart wanted to shout. They'd be working together, seeing each other every day. He'd talk, or he'd *listen*. After she'd gotten some sleep, she'd conjure the words.

That was the one good thing about becoming Lia again. She'd been Ophelia while at home in Portugal, and that had taken time to adjust to, too. She'd remember how to be Lia. Lia, who always had opinions and wasn't afraid to share them. And maybe by the time she left Antarctica, she'd figure out who she really was, outside the judging eyes of people who had expectations of her.

Sleep would help. Being around her best friend again would help her remember Lia, the version of herself she preferred to the sober, sad child she'd been.

"Lia?"

She hadn't heard anyone approach, but the sound of her name in her best friend's voice pulled her eyes open again. Once again, she saw anger in the eyes of someone she loved, but this time, it wasn't directed at her.

"What did he say?" Jordan demanded, grabbing her in a quick, hard hug that grounded her enough to banish church aisles and promises of forever from cluttering up her ability to speak.

What had he said?

"Nothing," Lia muttered, making her arms contract, giving an underachieving hug in return. "He said nothing."

When Jordan leaned back, her scowl had grown deeper, firmer. "What did you say to him? Did you tell him he's the world's smallest man and you hoped global warming would eventually thaw out his glacial heart? Would be the only good thing to come from it."

Jordan with the better zingers than Lia, despite the months of practice and mental composing she'd done.

Lia just shook her head, no heart for it. "I didn't say anything. I wasn't expecting to see him yet."

"I was going to tell you. I arranged it so he couldn't get too far away if he wanted to sleep at all while he's here."

"That's his cabin?"

Jordan nodded, but one glance over her shoulder to the door showed her hesitation. "Maybe I shouldn't have done that. Or maybe I shouldn't have even told you he was here."

The worry in Jordan's voice and eyes helped her get some clarity.

"Nonsense. I want to be here. It's cold, but I'll get used to it. I just need to think of what to say before—"

"You have some time."

Ten days. Something she'd reminded herself at least ten thousand times on the trip down. "I was just about to drop my bags off and go to the clinic, as directed."

"And he was just standing there?" Jordan took the bags and the keys, and opened the door to lead Lia into what she would've called a closet under any other circumstances. A small closet. With a small bed.

"With the expression of someone who'd be packing as soon as possible and taking the first transport out."

Something she could appreciate as she mentally inventoried the tiny room. Two windows wrapping around the corner, as the cabin sat at the end of the pod. Twin bed. Bedside table. And a built-in wardrobe that might have actually been a cupboard. Half a meter area to walk from door to window and everything else to the right against the wall.

Cozy.

That's what she decided right then to call it. Yep. Cozy. A small space that would be easier to keep warm. There, some optimism.

"He looks at me like that every day," Jordan confirmed, placing the suitcases by the bed and gesturing Lia back out. "Well, not exactly like that, but we'll talk more about what a louse he is later. I'm not just the welcome wagon, I'm supposed to show you to your physical."

A physical she didn't need but understood the reason for. As they walked back the way she'd come, Jordan filled up the empty space where Lia still had no words, chattering on about the station and the job. And Zeke. Jordan's trip to the southernmost continent had led her to meet and fall in love with someone she may have never met otherwise. Lia would just be happy to meet the true Lia, not some version she'd learned to present, depending upon her audience.

"You won't go into the schedule until tomorrow," Jordan continued, walking Lia back the way she'd come. "I was going to ask if you wanted to have dinner tonight, but as tired as you look, I'm thinking you might just want to sleep."

That wasn't all she wanted, but it would probably facilitate her being able to think well enough to do the other thing: grab West by the beard and shake some answers out of him. Not that she had the energy for that, either.

"Play it by ear?"

"You got it. After I introduce you to Zeke…"

* * *

Every muscle in West's body ached by the time he made it to the clinic. How he'd gotten there, he couldn't say. One second, he was watching his second biggest regret catch up with him, the next he stood in the lobby of the medical center with his head buzzing and no idea why he'd even come.

What the hell was she doing there? He should've turned around and left Fletcher the moment he'd arrived and found Jordan Flynn stationed there. With her, it assured Lia would learn of his location. If he'd had any idea she'd come all that way, he wouldn't have stayed. When it came to Lia Monterrosa, he was weak. The only way he could see to giving her a better life, not ruining it as he'd ruined Charlie's, was to leave. Leaving had been the only way for them to both survive; he couldn't go through that kind of loss again.

Without him there, she could move on and find someone more deserving than a man who couldn't even hear her name without remembering the day, months earlier, when he'd had to claim the body of his little brother. Someone who would still be alive if it weren't for West's ultimatum. Not that it took hearing her name, or thinking of her, to be sucked right back there. It could barely be called a memory; it remained so present in his head it was like one long, unending day since.

He'd assumed once Jordan delivered the news, they'd both curse him and do whatever women did when thousands of miles separated them but there was an ugly breakup to contend with.

She hadn't been going to his cabin. She'd carried luggage, and worn the standard-issue red snowsuit given to every crew member.

She'd been moving into the empty cabin beside his. And he'd just stood outside his door because…

He rubbed between his brows, trying to will some clarity to his thoughts.

It wasn't morning. He'd...gone to the shop for supplies, then the post office to collect books he'd ordered a month ago, and...that was why he'd even been there. Dropping off his packages. After lunch. Which meant he was in the clinic because he had physicals to perform for the six new arrivals who the department head had put on the schedule a week ago: four scientists, a computer programmer and the doctor hired to overwinter.

Lia was there for the winter. The woman who lived for sunshine had signed up for six months of Antarctic night?

Whatever.

He wasn't staying on. He just had to hold on for the next ten days without groveling and begging her to forgive him. Even through the horror darkening the edges of his vision, his whole body sparked, and he breathed too fast. He needed to slow that down before someone came in.

Regardless of the constant state of chill in the station's open facilities, he felt sweat running down his spine, and did the only thing he could—ripped his jacket off and hung it on the wall hooks.

Damn it. The clinic was the last place he should be. Walking away from her just now had only hit the pause button on whatever she'd come to say. He just needed a minute to think.

Focus.

He walked to the counter at the wall where hard backups of patients' files were kept, and braced his hands on the counter for stability, then closed his eyes and took a deep, slow breath.

Get it together. With his current state of mental function, almost nothing permeated the towering brick wall cutting across his brain. He'd be useless like this if there was an emergency.

He never let himself picture what it would be like to see her again, but if he had, it wouldn't have been gut-churning. Leaving wiped the slate, let him have a start fresh. Always. And once he'd gotten past that big first hump, the pain of loss dulled. Sometimes slower than others.

The thought of her projected her sorrow-filled expression on that towering wall in his head. Sad. Heartbroken, even. But not angry. She'd obviously come to see him, but hadn't come out swinging. Something wasn't right.

"West." His name spoken jerked his attention back to earth and he turned to see the medical director, Dr. Tony Bradshaw, approaching, folders in hand. "The new arrivals—"

"I know," West cut in, shaking his head, "you told us days ago."

The man was getting so forgetful, West should be so lucky. And too thin, but he didn't comment on that. They'd had that conversation twice before, and there was only so much West could do to make the man accommodate the increased metabolic needs Antarctica triggered.

He took another slow breath, fighting his own body, depriving himself of the increased demands for oxygen through sheer force of will.

"Right," Tony said slowly, as if he truly didn't remember, and handed over the folders. "Jordan is coming in to help you. She went to round some of them up."

Went to round up Lia.

She'd just stopped outside his door, with eye contact that pulled at him like gravity, and dragged memories into the front of his mind. The way she smelled fresh from the shower. Or better, first thing in the morning when she had his scent all over her, and it all mingled together. His cabin didn't smell like home still.

The sudden heat returned, and he noticed the inconsistency of it—the whole front of him on fire, and his spine like an ice core down his back, a frozen ice dagger digging into the base of his skull. Twisting. Tangling the nerves there, spaghetti-style.

"I've got a meeting, so you and Jordan sort them out," Tony called from the door as West bent to gather up the paper he'd dropped.

"Right."

He sighed hard enough to waft paper off the top of the pile.

Just get through the next couple of hours. That was the only thing to do.

Then she could go back home now and management would have time to get another doctor in there, someone suited to the winter, and he wouldn't have to spend the next eight months thinking about her and wondering if the woman who lived in the sunshine was all right with the unending dark of Antarctic night. He needed a fresh start. Another fresh start.

"You all right?" Tony's voice came from behind him, still there. Not gone.

And still no answer to give. At least, that he wanted to give. Far from all right. He hadn't been all right for months, why should today be better?

"Not sleeping great," he said. It was the only thing he could think of that wasn't a lie.

"Are you taking the sleep aids?"

"Aye." He stood. If they were going to talk about his health, he'd say something again about Tony's. The man was going to overwinter to head some project for NASA, and his weight loss would become more of an issue soon. "You still tryin' to increase calories? You're too thin."

Tony dropping inches was more of an issue than West's sleep troubles.

Tony redirected, ignoring his question. "Get Jordan to do a thyroid check on you when you're done with the newbies."

"Checked last week, man." West reminded him about that, too, refusing the redirect. "You do the same. Forgetfulness is a T3 symptom."

"Fine, fine."

Which meant *no*.

"Threw me straight out of the bunk." Jordan's voice came from the door providing the interruption Tony needed to slip out. He heard Lia's voice in reply and had to force himself not to look at her until his thundering heart slowed.

That was one thing he had going for him with this—no matter how riled up, Lia was a quiet talker. If she insisted on having it out with him, he could get her into a treatment bay, close the door, and whatever she had to say to him wouldn't carry through the walls. So long as he kept *his* voice down. The walls between the cabins were paperthin, but not in the medical center.

But that would entail giving Lia a physical... The thought shouldn't make that heat burrowing into his chest grow, dip lower, grow hotter. The very last thing he should do was touch her in any capacity. It would snowball. It always snowballed. He had no restraint around her. Even wanting to avoid the conversation he knew was coming, he still wanted to look at her. He still wanted to touch her.

He picked up the stack of folders and turned to find both Jordan and Lia watching him. Waiting for him to say something. Too bad.

A quick sort of the folders, and he handed three to the other doctor, making sure Lia's was on top.

"Tony wants everyone done ASAP."

Jordan shared a look with Lia, but took the folders.

"If you're planning to ignore me the rest of your time at the station, get ready to be annoyed." Lia finally spoke, soft voice, pointed words.

It was still the three of them, waiting on the arrival of the rest of the new crew. He could risk saying something short. He just didn't know what to say, other than a direct response or ignoring her.

"I'm already annoyed."

He finally let himself look at her again, holding her gaze for a second before the curious presence of pink on her head had him looking up, and then down over her, cataloging differences between the woman before him and the one he'd known in London.

Tired. Tanned. Pink hat. She hated pink. Wispy brunette curls poked out from beneath the folded brim, longer than the short, edgy pixie she was known for. The effect was the same, drawing all focus to her soft, feminine features.

"Welcome to my life," she said, words still softly spoken in her usual custom, but with steel he'd never been able to resist. Strength he'd long admired. Strength he'd once upon a time pictured in her as the mother to his children. The kind of mother like he'd never experienced, and which might not even exist. A mother who would fight and die to protect her children.

Another life. Another future he'd failed to build.

"You seriously want to do this here?"

She didn't answer him. A couple of seconds passed, and she just turned to Jordan. "Can you do mine first? I'm the only one here, and I'm really tired from the trip. It's amazing I'm upright."

Shutting him out was fine. Shutting him out was perfect.

Showdown at least momentarily averted, he headed off to the side of the room where he could spread the files on the countertop for review. It gave him something to do. He'd take anything that dulled the knife at his neck, and helped him ignore the pull she exuded. It was all he could do.

CHAPTER TWO

ONCE WEST HAD made a decision he did his best to move on it. Over the hours between Lia's arrival and the dragged-out end of his shift, he'd decided the only way to handle things was to tackle his Lia problem head-on, as brutally as his conscience would allow.

The circumstances of his shift only served to wrench up his irritation—two of his three assigned physicals had showed up, but the third, a recalcitrant astrophysicist, had ignored multiple calls to the telescope. Then, five minutes before the end of his shift, an emergency bone-setting had dragged his shift out an extra hour.

By the time he made it to her cabin door, some of his gut-swirling panic had settled into annoyance, and he let it. Was glad for it. Annoyance helped keep fond memories at bay. He didn't need anything making him want to go to her, talk to her, make her smile. Kiss her. Even if he could drum up anger for her, he doubted he'd still want to be outside of her presence. Ever.

The only way to handle this was to make sure she didn't want him, make sure she hadn't come all the way to Antarctica to try and reconcile. Make sure she understood they were done.

Remove temptation.

He had to, harsh and quick, like a battlefield surgeon

removing a gangrenous limb so the person would live. Only he was also the limb.

He took a deep breath to wrest control back from the willful, stubborn and half-wild, survival-focused part of his personality, and knocked.

Get the words out, move on. If she didn't want him, he wouldn't have to fight his own impulses for the next ten days. Not the best plan, but the only one he had.

He listened for signs of movement within. If she was there, he'd hear her.

Seconds ticked on, but no sound came from inside the tiny room. He knocked again, louder.

Then he heard the sound of bedclothes rustling, and when the door opened, her sleepy, confused face appeared in the frame. Four hours of frustration, but when he looked at her, memories of their mornings together and that old affection wrapped around him, making him want to wrap around her. Pretend now was then, and at any second, the sleepy confusion would warm to one of those soft-eyed smiles he'd so adored. The glimpses she'd reserved for him, past her strength, competency or expectations, to see the woman within.

But when her confusion cleared, there was nothing soft in her eyes for him.

Good. He did his best to ignore the exhaustion in her eyes, in her whole body.

"I'll make it quick," he said, gesturing inside with a nod. "Tomorrow."

He finally noticed in the dim light that she was wearing pink from head to toe. Some fluffy pink thing. Pajamas, maybe. It had a hood and feet built in. His annoyance had already started to fade.

Why was she wearing pink everywhere? She hated pink. Lord, he wanted to ask. But that would be showing an interest, the opposite of what he was trying to do. So would touching her, even though the urge to feel her skin against his boomed through him like a foghorn.

"Now or never, Lia." He curled his fingers to his palms with the control it took not to push the door in, haul her to him. Just looking at her hurt.

Hell.

"Speak now, or forever hold your peace?" She spoke softly, like the effort to utter every word shaved a year off her life.

The ceremonial words sailed straight and true, and hit harder than a sledgehammer. Despite his determination to be a stone, he couldn't hide the shock rippling through him, but grit his teeth, nodded once, and she stepped back to let him in.

This was why he didn't stick around to watch the destruction after whatever life catastrophe had triggered. He couldn't stand there, inside the bubble of pain he could almost see around her, warping reality. As if this cabin were some awful place that existed between two universes, the one where he'd gotten everything he'd ever wanted, and this one, where the last gift he could give her was walking away.

He closed the door behind him and leaned there, while she tracked the measly few feet that made up the whole of the walking space, getting as far from one another as was possible in the tiny space.

In his mind, all afternoon, when he'd pictured himself coming, acting it out, he'd dialed his performance to eleven. Shouted. Said ugly, awful things. Lied. Everything he could think of to make her angry, to make her hate him. But there with her, breathing the same air, feeling the pain written all over her, from the tilt of her eyebrows to the way she shifted from foot to foot, fidgeting, her hands hidden in her cuffs, he couldn't do it.

He couldn't do it, more proof that he had to make her want to stay away.

He forced himself to look her in the eye, but kept his voice quiet, and more sympathetic than he wanted. "I don't know what you're wantin', lass, but you're wastin' your time comin'. It's done between us. Over. Say what you want to say, and let's have done with it."

He heard his accent thicker than it had been in years, not just the shifting pronunciation, but the words, the cadence. Further proof this was scrambling his eggs.

"I didn't come to *say* anything. I wanted to see with my own eyes that you were alive and well." Her voice wobbled, like it had to pass through bubbles of emotion in her throat. This would be easier if she would just shout.

"And now you see."

"Alive. And I need to understand why the man who said he loved me, the only—" She stopped midthought, and closed her eyes, hands slipping from her sleeves enough to fidget before her as she struggled for composure. "Why would you just leave without word, three days before our wedding? I deserve to know what I did wrong."

There it was, her taking the blame for it. An example of exactly what she would do if he told her the whole damned story, try to take his guilt away or at least share the load. She'd probably say his brother had committed suicide because she'd taken too much of West's time, or that it was her fault because she was the subject of West's ultimatum. He couldn't have an addict around his new family, and he'd picked Lia over Charlie. And Charlie had picked drugs over rehab and family. A choice Charlie obviously wasn't ready to make, and he should've seen that. If he'd listened…

He lifted one hand to mash against his forehead, trying to rub away the tension headache already starting to drill in.

Don't think about Charlie.

He didn't need to explain. He wasn't *going* to explain. But if he wanted her to believe him, not take the blame, he had to give some excuse. Pinning some action on her would be an even greater sin than the lie he was about to tell. He couldn't make her take the blame. He'd take it. He deserved it.

"You didn't do anything wrong." The muscles all seemed to have tightened, and making his mouth form words was harder than running in water. "Something happened, and I needed to go. So I left."

"What happened?"

"I don't want to talk about that. I don't want to talk about any of this, and you know that."

Her shoulders bobbed quickly under the fluffy pink onesie she'd zipped herself into. In any other circumstances, the ridiculousness of her outfit would delight him—with the hood and the footsies attached—but he hadn't smiled in a long time.

"I don't care about your aversion to talking about the past. It's not that far in the past, and I need to understand."

"Aye, I see that. But you don't need to know everything. You're not part of my life now, Lia. We're not friends. We're not lovers. We're not engaged."

"If you had to leave, I would've gone with you."

"No," he said swiftly, searching for any route that would get through to her. "When I proposed, I thought it was love. I thought I loved you. Turns out, I didn't."

The color drained from her face.

"But when I left…" she started, but then just stopped. Like she didn't even have an avenue to try and argue it. Like it was almost expected.

Which it probably was. He had left her days before their wedding.

That was something he should apologize for; he could do that without explanations. But softening his position now would be a bad idea. Inside, he was already as soft as peat; it wouldn't take much for him to sink into the dreck. He'd apologize another day, after she'd accepted things.

"Is there anything else you want to discuss?"

Speak now, or forever hold your peace... She didn't even have to say the words this time.

"I guess I don't have anything else to say," she said, the words hanging there, sucking the air out of the room as she extended her left arm a bit, eyes fixed on the hand she'd let slide out from the cuff she'd tucked it into for warmth. "Just..."

He followed her gaze down to her hand. And the glittering diamond ring still perched on her finger. Where he'd slid it almost a year before.

The ice he'd felt cramming into the back of his neck earlier returned, a single, hard throb in his head stopping him from saying anything else. Why would she still be wearing that?

"I came to give this back." Her voice wobbled, then cracked, the sound as sudden and startling as a gunshot. "This beautiful ring we designed together, and the lie that it represents..."

Lia had other things she wished she had the strength to say, but as soon as she got feeling back in her face, she might be able to be proud of herself for still breathing after having him say the worst thing he could have to her. But all she could think of was to return the ring.

She flexed her hand, noted the way it trembled, the way her body could respond while mentally she still scrambled for anything to say. Her heart rabbited away. She heard her breath as if through a stethoscope, but it was as if every part of her brain was focused on keeping her upright and breathing. All emotion. No reason.

West stared at the ring, his jaw bunched and his brow beetled, but he didn't say anything.

Take it off. She was supposed to take it off now.

Forcing her arms to move, she latched on to the exquisite trigold engraved band and pulled.

In the first days, when she hadn't been able to locate him, the ring had been a comfort to her. When she discovered his empty flat, she'd clung to the promise she'd still trusted in and wanted to protect.

Her hands were cold enough that the knuckle, which always snagged it, had contracted, and it took nearly no effort for the ring to pop free. But everything still wobbled. Her hands. Her voice, when she finally found some words, the last she hoped she'd ever have to say to him. "I can't carry it anymore, or the weight of your broken promises."

The last word was whispered, no strength left to fake, all swept away with the sudden, sickly warmth washing over her face and down. Lightly stinging in her eyes and cheeks, then like a fever in her throat where muscles tensed, opened, hollowed so that when she breathed in it sounded strangled, choking…

Oh, no…

She was going to cry. As if she needed one more ounce of humiliation. The cascade of physical processes had already begun, the ones she could feel and which let her know it was too late to stop.

She thrust her hand out to him, the ring on her quaking palm.

He started to say something, but stopped dead a split second before her chin began the quiver and tears spilled.

Focusing on the process of it was the only thing she could think to do.

Useless Science Fact Number One: tears from grief and

pain were chemically different from those summoned by dirt or onion fumes.

Useless Science Question Number One: How would these tears have dried on a microscope slide? Spiky or like a web of fractals, like that strange theory she'd once read which hypothesized that different tears produced different crystalline salt structures.

She looked away from his eyes, not wanting to see him through the wavering watery line, or the horror there. But that coping mechanism fritzed and she had to reach for any other information to sedate her emotions.

"Lia?"

What else?

Something…

Prolactin.

Useless Science Fact Number Two: prolactin was somehow present in tears—a hormone initially believed only to govern lactation and the reason babies instinctively suckled. There was no way to stop it.

"Lia?" He said her name again, confusion present in his voice. As if she shouldn't experience grief. Like she wasn't a human who'd gone through loss in the past, who wasn't having her third round of grief in a handful of months, just because he'd wanted to share those old pains with her, or know her. Never wanted to let her close enough to love her, just close enough to fool her into thinking she'd finally found someone who would.

Lia never cried.

Ophelia had, but only when she was alone. She needed to be alone now.

He said her name again, but she could only shake her head, her eyes fixed on the little closet at his shoulder.

Why was he still standing there? Didn't he have any decency? Couldn't he see that she…

The ring. He hadn't taken it; she still felt it weighing her palm down.

When she gave it to him, he would go…

She thrust it forward, finally looking again at his face, his horrified face.

Enough. He had to go.

She opened her mouth to tell him, but a short, choked hiccup came out instead, and in her own horror, she slammed her free hand over her mouth to hold it.

"Lia?"

He had to stop saying her name like he could make her stop feeling by him being horrified by it.

One step forward came with his word this time, so her knuckles touched his chest.

The brush of his hand on her well-padded arm got through the grief fogging her brain.

He thought he could be horrible and cruel and then just…what? Comfort her? Maybe tell her to stop being dramatic?

No.

She peeled her own hand from her mouth and slapped his hand away hard. Then again, because it wasn't far enough. She'd come all this way, and now all she wanted was distance.

Distance and getting rid of the ring, which he still hadn't taken. A quick survey of his attire provided an array of pockets where she could stick the cursed thing. She found one, and as soon as she'd stuffed the diamond band inside, she shoved at his chest.

"Lia, you have to take a breath. Calm down."

"Stop saying my name." She panted the words, because she was only half functioning on intention.

"Okay, but you have—"

"Get out!"

West lifted both hands, palms forward, to stay her, and backed warily out the door.

As soon as he stepped through, she took two big steps, made sure it was as closed as possible, then flipped the locks.

She crawled back into bed and pressed her face into the pillow to muffle the sounds she couldn't stop.

It was done. It was over. She'd wanted to know what she'd meant to him, and now she knew. But she'd always known that, in the back of her mind. She'd just let herself pretend otherwise.

CHAPTER THREE

WEST PUSHED INTO the clinic early the next morning, before anyone else had arrived, and flipped on the lights before heading straight for the supply room.

He'd endured many sleepless nights when he'd first arrived at Fletcher Station, but with the absence of dark, there was a healthy insomniac population for him to blend into.

Last night, he'd been unable to will away the image of her with tears on her cheeks, the complete breakdown of the steel-framed woman he'd known. In the moment, he thought he'd heard everything she'd said to him; he'd tried to listen, but it wasn't there in his head. All the times he'd concentrated, pressed the mental replay, all he got was the vision of her shaking and crying, and the understanding that it would take a long time to scab over.

Worse, he couldn't shake the notion that he'd ruined her as badly as he'd ruined Charlie. Yet more proof that he shouldn't be trusted with the psychological well-being of anyone.

The only good thing a sleepless night afforded him was early breakfast and getting to lock himself away before she arrived for her first shift. If he was lucky, he could busy himself counting everything, a task that would minimize contact with other people, while staying mostly out of sight. For her.

Instinct said *give her time*. Trust Jordan to be there for her to lean on as he was sure she had done at the start. But it also said *keep an eye on her*. Because he just wasn't sure how bad this could get. He prayed not as bad as it had with his brother, but then Lia wasn't an addict. She had Jordan looking out for her. Maybe he should quietly ask her to keep a closer eye…

He opened the digital inventory and sent it to the office printer. Working on paper would be easier on his fried brain, and anything he could do to make today easier, he would. Including throwing himself into monotony, testing the status of everyday machines used for testing and upkeep. Centrifuge, autoclave and irradiator for sterilizing equipment that would be reused—something he'd never encountered in any other hospital but was in Antarctica. Everything brought onto the continent had to be shipped out again, including all forms of garbage.

He left in nine days.

"Are we having fun yet?" Jordan asked after throwing away the last bits of a stitch kit Lia had used on a butter-fingered galley cook, her second patient of the day.

As part of her first day on the job, Lia shadowed Jordan to learn her way around and get a crash course in station medicine, which was like some cross between a small hospital and field medicine. "Oh, sure, nothing like stitching up a hearty thumb slice to get the party started."

"Or an asthma attack."

"That was the first party of the day," Lia corrected her thumb party joke, finishing up the file entry for the thumb.

She'd expected to struggle to find the old Lia, the version of her that Jordan knew, but a few minutes with her almost maid of honor had her stepping into London Lia's shoes once more, the ones she hadn't been strong enough to cram onto her metaphorical feet with West last night.

Not that she had to try too hard in that regard. Of all the people in her life, Jordan, who'd known her since medical school, was the most likely to be accepting of changes to the Lia she knew. But it was just one more thing on an already overwrought mind and Lia didn't have it in her yet to try and sort out who she was supposed to be while trying to sort out everything else. While still hollow and cold from last night's official breakup. Breakdown. Whatever. From feeling him very close by, but knowing she wouldn't be welcome if she spoke to him, that she shouldn't even want to speak to him, that he'd never smile for her again or cuddle under a warm woolly blanket with her to watch some silly movie with more special effects than story.

If being London Lia made it even a tiny bit easier, she'd stick to it for now. But that didn't mean she couldn't tell Jordan the truth about her situation, it just meant she had to be strong about it. No matter how helpless and heartbroken she might be on the inside.

"But I guess this is just my life now."

"While you're here, you mean?" Jordan asked, her tone saying she'd picked up on the undercurrent of dismay. "It can get more exciting here. Fieldwork can be pretty dangerous—not that you'll be doing any of that over the winter. Are you nervous about staying?"

"For the winter?" Lia popped her head out of the treatment room to make certain no other patients had come in while they stood there chatting. "Not really. I've decided it's adventurous and as my life is no longer going to be neurosurgery exciting, and even if my cabin is freezing compared to the rest of the station, it's adventure time and I should enjoy the memory-making."

"I'm going to come back to that whole life-without-adventure thing, but right now…your cabin was really that cold last night?" Jordan asked. "Inside the station never seems much colder than being at home."

She had a point. Lia didn't feel colder in the clinic, but no, her cabin had been colder. "Maybe I was just really tired. But honestly, I was always a little bit cold when I worked in London, and that was before I spent time in Portugal. Maybe the warm temperate climate had made me go soft."

Jordan snorted her disbelief, a testament to how well Lia had played the self-assigned role of all things unsinkable. "You'll do more than waste away in a little village. Maybe you can work part-time in Porto."

All Lia could think to do was nod. "Maybe."

But even if the authorities were still unsure if her father would return and take over the vineyard, she wasn't confused about it. Once he lost interest in something, that was it. Her mother. His second and third wives. Her—not that she could remember him ever having interest in her. Just the opposite. Disappointment that she wasn't male, and all the assurances that she'd never inherit. A point that had left her further confused when the lawyers had said, with him gone, she was the one indicated in his paperwork to manage Monterrosa Wine.

But that strange surprise had faded when they'd informed her that as soon as she married it would be her husband who actually inherited the vineyard. At that time, she'd thought that would be West. Now she might never feel comfortable enough to marry, not if she could be as wrong about West as she had been. A man who wanted her to believe he loved her? She'd probably fall for it without a drop of sense.

"But considering the village is called Monterrosa, I feel my first responsibility is to them, the people who have been loyal to Monterrosa Wine since the time of titles."

"Who was assigned Nigel Gates yesterday?" The question came from the lobby area, immediately shifting both of their attention from the spiky conversation.

"Tony?" Lia mouthed the question to Jordan, not yet able to identify people by voice.

Jordan nodded, then mouthed back, "West had him."

They both eased off the counter where they'd been leaning and drifted out to the lobby in time to see West coming out of the room where the autoclave and irradiators lived.

"I had him, but he never showed. It's in the file," West said, glancing toward the two of them, but focusing again on the medical director. "I was here with a broken arm an hour after end of shift, and he never made an appearance. Called up to the BAT twice before that, no answer."

Nigel was being uncooperative. Figured.

"BAT?" she whispered to Jordan, staying out of the conversation between Tony and West, despite staying to listen in.

"Big-ass telescope," Jordan filled in. "There are a lot of goofy acronyms around here."

Lia nodded, but as it now all made sense, she had to join in the conversation. She could be an adult about this. She had to learn how to coexist with West at the station for several more days, couldn't spend the whole time avoiding him.

"Nigel is in a big hurry to get the telescope calibrated before the night sky appears. I guess it takes a lot of time and effort," she said, because she had picked up that much from the man's single-minded but strangely nonconversational conversation. "He's not going to take time away from that telescope without being forced."

"Why do you say that?" West asked, his voice growing quiet and sober enough that she had to look at him.

"We spent two days traveling with each other, talking and getting to know one another." Even if it was more like she was just there, listening to him talking to himself about his plans, she'd heard enough. "He's got a fire in his belly."

She immediately heard how it sounded—like she and

Nigel had developed more of a connection than they had, and while seeming less pathetic, like someone who was still able to connect to another man appealed, West only had to meet Nigel to know how inaccurate that assumption would be.

"What's the goal? A study of some kind?" Tony asked from the doorway of his office where he continued to loiter.

She could only shake her head. "I couldn't tell you. He told me. In detail. But it was more like me listening to him thinking out loud than conversation. I mostly understood his drive. He said he'll never get this kind of unrestricted access to a large telescope again, and his future plans ride on proving some theory. He's not coming out of there without pressure. And it'll probably get worse once the night sky arrives."

West moved on. "I'll call up there again, and if he doesn't answer, I'll take equipment and go."

The way he turned his body away from her made it clear her part of this conversation was over, and she turned to Jordan, and tried to pretend she didn't see worry in her friend's eyes.

West got on the radio, and after a moment, he was speaking into the mic, calling Nigel by name, but no response came but static and silence.

"He can hear it broadcasting over the whole building?"

"It's basically a big dome with a room built on for entry. If he's with the telescope, he should be able to hear the radio."

And why would he answer West today when he hadn't yesterday?

She stepped away from Jordan and, although the last thing she should do was get close to West, stopped a couple feet down from where he stood with the radio. "Let me try. He might answer me."

A few moments after she made the call and announced who it was, Nigel answered.

"Lia, busy right now." He mumbled something else, something about cycling and whatever that was, but it was an opening.

"It's really important that I get your baseline and type your blood, just in case there is some kind of emergency this winter and we're all cut off from evacs. Maybe you can make up the time later."

"Time is fixed, it cannot be made up."

"Okay, but it can be saved. If I get dinner delivered to you later, you won't have to come down to the galley and take time away, just keep working."

He was silent a moment, and then agreed, "Fine. But be quick."

Right. She rang off and then looked back to Jordan. "Want to come with me?"

Jordan nodded, but West interrupted, stepping over to take the radio from her hand. "He's my patient. I'm going. You don't need to go. Just send the dinner later."

"If he's going to be a problem child for the winter," Tony interjected, "Lia needs to reinforce her relationship with him and learn where to find him when he refuses to come down."

West's answering grunt had all eyes on him, but he *stared* at Lia for several long seconds before he nodded. "Lia can come with me if she wants to."

She definitely didn't want to, but she also didn't want to let him keep affecting all her decisions, making her less than she had the potential to be, as she'd been since she'd found him missing.

One look around provided a befuddled-looking Tony Bradshaw, who clearly did not understand the angsty undercurrent flowing between them all, but didn't ask for clarification. He just gave final directions about blood typing and equipment, then returned to his office.

"Get your boots on and your outdoor suit," West directed, then pivoted to grab a bag from the wall and headed for the inventory room again, where he'd been all day. "Meet me here in fifteen."

Right. Great.

She looked over to find Jordan hurrying to her side. "Are you sure you're okay with this? It probably shouldn't be all three of us, but if you don't want to make the trek alone with him, you can bow out and I'll take you up there tomorrow. So you know where it is."

The question alone would've alarmed Lia back home, but here it just confirmed that she wasn't pulling off her quiet strength act as well as she'd used to, no matter how easy it was to talk to Jordan again.

"It's okay. I said I was after adventure, right?"

"Yes, but I'm not sure spending time with *him* means adventure, just…suffering." Jordan kept her words quiet, and the gentle assertion of support had that tingling returning to Lia's eyes. She shook her head and gestured to the door, eager to escape before that awful leaking came back. "I need to get my suit. It'll be fine. I'm not going to let him make me dread any part of my adventure. I'm here to revel. R.E.V.E.L. And climbing a frozen, snowy, almost-mountain is the kind of adventure I can't have in Portugal. Don't worry."

She silently repeated the words to herself. Don't worry. Don't worry because he couldn't say anything worse than he already had. And that stare of his hadn't said he wanted to talk to her about anything, just like him hiding out in the storage room all day said he didn't want to be in her presence any more than she wanted to be in his.

"I'm going to worry, anyway," Jordan muttered, still looking uneasy with the concept, but apparently with enough confidence in Lia still to say, "Call me for dinner when you get back. Zeke and I will meet you in the galley."

"Okay. Don't worry," she repeated. "We're just going to work. Said everything we needed to last night."

"You did?" If possible, Jordan looked more alarmed.

Suddenly, Lia didn't want to uphold any masks with her. She could shrug it off, she would've before, but she probably couldn't pull off the unaffected face. Not when she knew that her eyes were still a little red, which might become a chronic condition.

"I don't think I can talk about it yet," she said after a hard pause that made a little line appear between Jordan's brows.

Jordan squeezed her hand once and nodded, accepting. "When you're ready."

She had to swallow down another rise of emotion, but glanced toward the door. "If I'm late, he won't wait for me."

God knew West found it too easy to leave her behind.

CHAPTER FOUR

WEST STOOD AT the door of his cabin, a rigged heater in his arms, ready to take it next door to Lia.

She didn't know he was coming. Probably wouldn't want to see him at her door for the second night in a row, but he had to do something.

No matter how sound his reasoning, West knew he'd abandoned her. And he knew how bad that felt. How it wormed down into places you didn't even realize were there, and came out when you least wanted. Over the years he'd seen it from every angle—from the slow-motion abandonment of his mother, to Charlie's withdrawal into substance abuse, and even from the other side and the many times he'd walked away from friendships or half-formed relationships to outrun Charlie's problems.

Until Lia.

Until West had met Lia and was no longer willing to start over anywhere she wasn't. And in his fear of losing her, he'd hidden his biggest weakness from her—his addict brother. She knew he had a little brother, but he'd hidden the bad parts. To keep her from asking to meet Charlie, West had concocted a story about an adventure in the States, working his way across the continent, like some romanticized vagabond.

That was the first in a string of unforgivable sins that led him here.

If he'd told her the truth back then, he might have never felt the need to make Charlie choose. Or maybe he would've done it gentler, and actually listened to the words his brother said. West had heard *"Have a nice life"* as another passive-aggressive jab of guilt. It wasn't until much later that he'd understood it to have been a more final goodbye.

He needed to pay attention to Lia right now. Make sure she didn't have a Charlie reaction to his choices. She was still his responsibility, and if anything happened to her...

Not that he thought Lia suicidal, but he'd once thought her made of iron, stronger than anyone else he'd ever known. Strong or not, she'd still cried herself to sleep last night, and he'd heard every sniff and hiccup through the paper-thin cabin walls. He'd seen the evidence of it all day in her still-puffy eyes, and it ate at him.

He stepped out of his cabin, closed the door and took the two steps separating them to lightly knock on hers. Unlike last night, she didn't take long to respond.

With the door held half-open in front of her like a shield of protection, she met his gaze and some of the burning in his chest eased when she didn't flinch or look away. Of course, that meant he could see fresh redness in her eyebrows that contradicted the flash of strength. And still wearing the pink pajamas, but she hadn't been sleeping, at least not yet.

No greeting, no deep longing looks and no hope in her voice, she glanced at what he carried and back up. "Flower pots?"

"Heater," he said softly, tapping the terra-cotta pots with one finger. If the promise of heat didn't buy him admittance, he had no words to ask. No words for anything. There was a time when he'd always had something to say to her. Waited, saving up thoughts throughout the day to tell her at night. Stupid things to make her smile, or things to spark debate. Teasing. Challenging. Playful. But now, every word he uttered could give him away. He couldn't afford to overshare.

"How?"

"I'll show you. It'll warm the cabin, those at the end of the pods are exposed to more outside walls than those stacked side by side. They don't retain the heat as well."

She considered the pots for another several seconds, door still in place, then simply let go of the door and moved back inside.

He closed the door behind him, then wordlessly stepped to the bedside table to clear it off while she burrowed back into a mountain of blankets on the bed.

Explaining how the pots functioned as a heater while he assembled it was easy at least. He lit four tea-light candles for the bottom layer and stepped back to mention safety; even if she didn't need to hear not to touch hot things, it was easier.

"But I guess you don't need to be warned about the danger of fire."

"Not really," she muttered. "Things I need to be warned about never come with a warning. Or I'm just really bad at picking up on hints."

So was he. Charlie had proven that.

And she didn't need to know that. "Hints?"

"Do you really want to know?" she asked, pushing down the blankets to her lap so she could sit up straighter, but stayed tucked into the bed.

He was suddenly sure he didn't want to know, but he said, anyway, "Tell me."

One purposeful nod, and she asked, "When did you know you didn't love me? Because I've had months of wondering what happened while I was gone. The last thing you said to me at the airport that day was 'I love you.' Did I miss something? Did you know then?"

Hell.

No more circling the problem. This was more like the Lia he knew than the sad-eyed woman he'd seen every time he'd looked at her since she'd arrived.

And he didn't have an answer. He never considered that he'd need to have more of an answer.

"I figured it out after," he said. "Probably good you didn't want me to come to Portugal with you."

"What does that mean?"

"You didn't want me to go."

Her eyes narrowed. "Why would I invite you to Portugal when you had no idea what you were going to be walking into? Because what is going on there? It's a mess, above what you've probably realized."

"Mess how?" he asked. "What's going on at Monterrosa now? Are you avoiding going there?"

"That seems to be your MO, not mine. I don't run away from pain—apparently I run toward it." She nodded once to him, then pointed to the door. "I think we're done. I understand exactly where you're coming from. You didn't love me, you figured it out as soon as I was out of sight because something mysterious happened. I'm guessing she had red hair."

"Lia."

"I don't suppose I need more details." She waved a hand toward the door.

He didn't move. He was finally starting to feel a little hopeful that she would get over him, that he wouldn't ruin her, too. "Are you finally getting angry?"

"Is that good, too?"

"Yes," he immediately answered, maybe a little too loudly.

"Why?"

He lowered his voice a little and shook his head. "Because I hate seeing you with red eyes."

"Sorry I'm disappointing you by being human."

"The Lia Monterrosa I know wouldn't let—"

"Maybe that's the problem, then." She cut him off. "You *don't* know me. And I'm tired of cleaning up messes of the men who should've loved me, but didn't. You left me to call off the wedding, after I figured out you weren't coming back, and I waited up until the last minute. Nine days after my father burned down half of the estate and dropped off the face of the earth so I've had to clean it up for the hundreds of people who rely on the vineyard for their livelihoods. Then I had to cancel my wedding because my fiancé disappeared, too. It was a great week."

He hadn't thought about the timing back then, but now seemed a good time to ask, since all information about her emotional state was of value. "Did you get it repaired?"

"Does it matter?" she asked, then stretched out in the bed, rolling to face the wall. "Thanks for the heater. You're still a *babaca*."

Final words if he'd ever heard them; even if he didn't understand the actual last one, he could read between the lines. Jerk. Ass. Something like that. And a little bit angrier, thank God. Anger was fire, and fire meant the will to fight. That was better than just curling up and taking whatever life had thrown at her.

But staying out of her way as much as possible until it was time to go was the right call. He definitely should go on that day trip into the field tomorrow. Even one day of distance had to help.

"What're you doin'?"

The familiar cadence of West's nearly tamed brogue stopped Lia midstick.

She lifted her gaze from the butterfly needle she'd been fishing for a vein with at the crook of her elbow to see him in the doorway, leaning, rough from a prolonged field mission, still wearing the thick red thermal suit, large duffel bag hanging on his shoulder.

It had been three days since she'd last seen him. Three days since their really awesome and definitely not soul-crushing *discussion.* Of course he'd be the one to find her performing a sneaky blood draw on herself.

"Trying and failing to get some blood."

He dropped the bag outside the door and meandered into the small exam room. "Maybe because you're right-handed and trying with your left."

"I have tiny veins, they're hard to hit, and the best one is on the right elbow crook." She halfway withdrew the tiny butterfly needle again, tilted it slightly and pushed forward again, gritting her teeth. Somehow it hurt more having to watch the needle, and when she was doing the steering, she definitely had to watch.

He headed for the sink, washed his hands and stepped to her side. "Stop."

He didn't swat her hand, but she heard the reprimand coming as he pinched the butterfly above where she'd held it, and she let go.

"You just had panels run six days ago." Dr. Obvious held the needle still and used his free hand to lightly palpate the vein above, considering his next move.

"I know. I was there."

"You could've had Tony do this for you, or anyone else in the department."

"I know that, too."

He didn't try to press the needle into the vein again, just took it out and watched as absolutely nothing happened. No blood. No extra firmness when he prodded the vein, which would indicate she'd at least perforated it and would have an unholy bruise. Nothing.

"You didn't even hit it."

"I'm good with my left hand, but it kept rolling."

West cleaned the site and applied pressure, anyway, holding her elbow in one hand to keep her still.

Besides the single fingertip used to search for the vein, it was the first time he'd touched her directly, without fabric separating them, and seemingly subconsciously his fingertips all seemed to flex and move, caressing, massaging, stroking her skin far more than holding her still.

Even with all the crap between them, her heart rate kicked up and her gut gave a squeezing roll—somewhere between excited butterflies and nausea, enough to remind her how she *should* feel about him touching her. How she still didn't feel about him touching her, even after everything. Even after knowing it had only been love on her part.

And that, for some reason, when he realized he hadn't loved her, he no longer even wanted to try. He didn't want to keep going, see if his feelings developed. That was something else she didn't understand, how she went from being worth the effort and time all relationships required, to not.

"I don't need a massage," she whispered, shifting her gaze to her elbow so that he'd look that way, too, and it worked. He stopped, then frowned, let go and took one step back.

Then for good measure, he ran his hand, open-palmed, down the front of his suit, wiping the feel of her off, as if she were covered in goo.

"So why didn't you ask Tony?" he asked, like he had done nothing bizarre or insulting. "You're usually a play-by-the-rules type."

She couldn't help staring a little longer at the imaginary goo trail on his suit, but managed to answer, "I'm not a type."

In the time he'd been gone, she'd managed to build a little callus over the strips of flesh she felt carved off, but it was eggshell-thin. Almost an illusion. Maybe completely an illusion.

It was a lot of work to keep her emotions at bay with him there. The whole time he'd been gone, she'd been outside of the expectations of anyone who knew her—Jordan and Zeke were in the field, too—and she hadn't known how to react to anything, except that one core feeling of loss and grief. She didn't even know whether to be irritated by the emails with her consultants, or patient with them repeatedly questioning her decisions. But in that moment with him, it was perfectly clear. What she wanted to do was shout at him. To lash out, make him feel as bad as that one little motion made her feel. But she didn't want to give him the satisfaction.

"I didn't ask because I didn't want help. Also, I only decided after my last patient that I needed to do it."

He stood back a little, his eyes sharpening. "Are we on winter hours now?" He nodded through the door to the dark lobby.

"People have already started going home, and there were a number of medical staff out in the field."

"And you didn't want to wait until tomorrow," he filled in.

"Somehow I wasn't enthused with the idea of having one more thing on my mind all night."

A single nod was the answer and he asked, "Want me to do it?"

"If you can stand touching me."

The careful quiet way he'd been looking at her sharpened, then with one hand he cupped her cheek and leaned forward, urging her to meet him.

Her heart squeezed, but the thundering settled into a gentler gallop when he tilted his head and pressed a warm, slow kiss to her temple, where he lingered and softly spoke, "Don't do that. That's not what that was."

Another painful squeeze to her chest, and the gallop accelerated, but she lost track of her pulse in the tingling that radiated from wherever he touched her, and it came again, that stinging in her eyes she hated. A simple touch to remind her of what she'd lost.

When he let go and stepped back, his expression was softer, but his lips twitched before he made a comically exaggerated show of wiping his mouth on his sleeve, and then wiping his hand on her trousers, right down the thigh.

A little laugh puffed from her and she swatted his hand away, smiling over the dewiness in her eyes.

"Tell me what this is for." He nodded to the pale green stoppered vacuum tube, as if he needed to ask. He knew what panels were run on that particular tube, the preservatives at the end that varied by tube color—and, given their location, which test was most likely the one she was going for. He might lead in with the charm she'd thought frozen dead when he'd come to Fletcher, but he was still going to make her say it.

"I had a patient with Polar T3 symptoms, and decided that I might need another check on my thyroid, too."

He made some sound of affirmation, then began lightly prodding her one good vein, and still seeing no signs that she'd so much as grazed the sucker with her errant needle driving, he opened another needle, found the vein again, swabbed and then slipped it right in.

A minute later, it was over and she had a cotton ball bandage to stop the bleeding as he left for the lab room to get it started.

"I can take it from here." She followed him out, crooking her arm to apply pressure to the site.

"You're not treating yourself."

"It's not treatment, it's just a test," she argued. "And I'll be doing it for myself when everyone is gone."

"And if you already have dropping levels?"

She sighed, checked her stick location to make sure it wasn't oozing and then let her arm relax. "Cross that bridge when I get to it. You just got back from a long trip, you're tired."

"I'm fine to run this."

"Damn it, West, I don't want your help. I could've gone to my legs or something to get the blood—it was just easier to let you do it. Running the equipment isn't going to be affected by it being my own blood. I can do it just like I'd do for anyone else."

"Don't care," he grunted. "Better start thinking of the reasons you're going to give me as to why you felt the need to do another thyroid check six days after you had one."

"*I* know the reasons. That's enough."

He logged the samples while the machine got to work, turned to look at her. "Are you having trouble sleepin'?"

"No," she said swiftly, then shrugged. "A little."

"Mood swings?"

That was the one that got her, her absolute lack of emotional control the past several days. One minute she'd been glad West was gone, the next she was worried about him in the field. Not worried about Jordan, who wouldn't be back until the day before the big *boa viagem*. But West she'd worried about, and kind of hated him for that.

"I'm taking silence for *yes*."

"Yes." She echoed the word just so he'd stop looking at her like she couldn't take care of herself—she'd basically been looking after herself since she'd been released from her luxurious Portuguese penitentiary to the strange freedom of an exclusive girls' school in the States at sixteen. Not to mention her years at medical school, where she'd met Jordan, and then when they'd moved to London to work in the same hospital, where Lia had met West. "Mood issues are probably to be expected after all of *this*, don't you think?"

"Aye," he said softly, not rising to her bait.

"Still, I'd rather find out if it's physical or emotional as early as possible. And in case I'm just being paranoid, I didn't want to tell Tony. He's overwintering, too, will be the only other doctor here with me, and I don't want him to think I'm unstable or a hypochondriac, or that he should in any way doubt my abilities."

"Why would he doubt your abilities?" He unzipped the top of his snowsuit, proof that he'd just arrived back from their trip, and pulled it down to pool at his waist, baring his double layers of thermals. Because he'd basically been camping in subzero temperatures for several days.

"Why wouldn't he? Seems to be coming from several directions in my life right now. Personal fronts. Professional fronts. All my local foremen don't think it's right that a woman should *have* to run Monterrosa Wine. My father spent my whole life telling me I wouldn't inherit, but apparently changed his mind right before he left for parts unknown."

"Unknown? He's still gone?"

She nodded once, then checked to make sure the tiny puncture was no longer oozing, then slapped some tape over the cotton ball and rolled down her sleeve.

Change the subject.

"Did you sleep at all when you were out there?"

He nodded, but didn't answer out loud. He also didn't budge from the spot in front of the buzzing machine.

"And the cold?"

"There's a two-room building at the site—they go back to it every year. Has a stove and emergency supplies." He answered that probably because it was easier than all this emotional garbage. "No beds. Not meant for overnight stays. We'd have been back same day but for a storm that sprang up. Ended up glad for the emergency sleeping bags, even while we all slept on counters or the floor."

And he'd slept in those conditions. Amazing after him not having slept at all the night before he'd left, after their Awesome Talk. She'd barely slept, and he'd somehow managed to pace in a room with about two square meters of walkable space. The only proof she really had that he was still upset to see her, or upset in general. Might be about the mysterious something that sent him running to Antarctica, for all she knew.

Part of why she'd been glad to find his goodbye note hanging on her doorknob the next morning, if one could call a bag full of tiny candles that, or the scrap of paper that said, *For the heater while I'm gone*.

And he'd be truly gone soon. No matter how raw she still felt, she didn't want to spend the next few days bickering with him, or giving him an itemized list of all the wrongs he'd contributed to, leaving the way he did. He knew it had been the cruelest way to leave her; nothing she could say would make it as real for him as it was for her. She was the one...who shouldn't be in love anymore, but was having a hard time turning that off.

"Thanks for the blood draw," she said, because just telling him that she wasn't going to feel her feelings in a loud, outside-the-brain way anymore with him seemed weird. "If the levels are off, would you...slip the results under my door or something?"

"I'll come tell you," he said, and just as she'd nodded and turned to go, he said, "I don't doubt your ability or your worth. I'm sorry about your da'."

"Thanks," she said again, the only word she could think to say, and then hurried out. Food. Sleep. Maybe tonight was the night she'd crack open one of the two bottles of the family's finest vintages she'd swiped from the cellar before leaving. Seemed like a good night to force herself to sleep.

CHAPTER FIVE

LAST NIGHT HE'D made Lia Monterrosa smile at him, and every time he'd seen her today that had been all he'd been able to think about. Those brief seconds when her hazel eyes had warmed and his chest had filled with honey, thick and sweet, had been there all the time. Even in the smallest measurements, when they were midquarrel.

West stepped out of the line with his dinner tray, and seeing as the only tables with available seating held Lia—who was distracted and bent over her mobile phone—and Gates—who had the charisma of a dead rodent—he invited himself to sit with her.

Not that he should be so stupid, but that voice of pragmatism and self-preservation was getting quieter daily, and fading into the echo of how peaceful it had been to love her.

But even when his day trip had turned into three days and hundreds of miles had separated them she'd been on his mind.

"Do you mind?" he asked, placing his tray across the long narrow table from her.

Lia lifted her grumpy face—a look he recognized—but shook her head. "They say every twelve hours it passes over, and I thought that meant seven and nineteen, but here it is, ten minutes after and no signal."

Satellite. One of the difficulties with Antarctica was

moving there as a modern, urban human who'd grown used to easy access to the internet, Wi-Fi, mobile services… getting used to the change was hard. They only really got emails twice a day, unless the sender and receiver were both quick and focused enough to send and receive multiple emails within the forty-five or so minutes they had on each pass of the uplink.

"Waiting for an email?"

"Several. Manager. Consultants. Investigator. My father…" She grimaced lightly at the last.

He hadn't asked last night more questions after she'd confirmed that the man was still in the wind, but with this opening… "He's answering emails?"

"No. I just keep sending them." She put her device down and reached for her fork. "I meant the private investigators I've hired to try and track him down."

"They have news?"

She stopped eating, fork still in her mouth, the soft, pink slickness of her lower lip pressing to gently swell between the tines, her eyes wide and fixed on him.

"You don't have to talk about it. I was just making conversation." He shrugged, looked at her mouth again, dragged his gaze away, dropped to the table as other thoughts began swimming into his mind. Good thoughts. Wickedly good thoughts.

"You just never wanted to talk about that stuff."

True. Sort of. When it had been a danger that she'd start prodding around in things he didn't really want her knowing. "Did you sleep better knowing your T3 levels are fine?"

She watched him so closely that pragmatic voice turned a little paranoid, convinced she could see every prurient thought dancing across his mind just from the way he'd lamely fixated on her mouth.

After a weighty silence, she cautiously said, "I slept better than I would've had I been preoccupied with it." And then, "But I would've slept better still if there hadn't been a caged lion bunking next door, pacing."

West frowned at the idea they kept one another awake, then more deeply when he remembered the ways they'd once helped one another sleep. "I wasn't pacing."

And even if she'd just put off a vibe of not wanting to discuss things... "You were, but then you left the room and paced up and down the corridor for about a half an hour, where you probably growled and swiped at the air."

Demonstrably and adorably, she curled one hand like an ineffective claw and acted it out, swiping her paw while curling her upper lip into an exaggerated snarl.

He found himself smiling, that old chemistry still there. It had never needed too much prompting in the past. Affection he wanted to last, pretend that everything else wasn't there between them, no matter how stupid. Fall back into old habits before rings and tux fittings. "And you just laid there and listened?"

The phone momentarily forgotten, she still smiled, but as she watched him and considered her words, it began to diminish, growing smaller and then rueful.

"I laid there and worried actually." She waved one hand, as if to dismiss her own right to be worried. "Maybe you need to have *your* T3 checked."

The moment had passed, too hard for either of them to hold on to, and thrust them right back into spiky emotion territory, where neither knew what to do with any of it.

"I had it done the other day. This winter you should have Tony do yours. Keep up with it."

"I will. There was a grandparent with thyroid problems, I think. Of course, I could be misremembering. It's not as if my parents talked much with me about...well, you know."

"I know?" he repeated, and then shook his head. "Remind me."

"Anything besides studies and expectations? Then my mother died, and it was mostly about all the ways I disappointed by not having a penis."

It was the perfect opening for him to make a flirty joke, but he swallowed it down with his starchy meat stuff, which resembled what someone might think shepherd's pie was like, if they'd never eaten shepherd's pie, and only heard of it in stories.

The same way he knew about her parents, small scraps of information because he'd always wanted to look forward, to keep her looking forward. He didn't want to tell her about his mother, with her brassy, bottle-blond hair and too-red lips, or the last time he and Charlie had seen her. The neglect Lia seemed to have suffered was different, but still something they could've bonded over.

Just then, her phone pinged, then pinged again, over and over as emails began hitting her in-box. Her attention zeroed in there, reading and responding to emails, and not eating enough of her dinner. That he could legitimately comment on for her benefit.

"You need to eat more. People who overwinter tend to front-load the calories and try to put on some weight in the early part of the winter, because the last couple months are lean and it's better to have some cushion you can lose."

"I'll eat when I'm done," she said, but had clearly retreated from the conversation.

"Hey, you lot!" a man called from the double doors leading out of the galley. Lia and everyone else stopped talking, stopped eating, and heads swiveled in unison toward the man shouting for attention. "First aurora spotted on the horizon. Get your asses out there if you want to see them before you go home."

Aurora! The perfect timely reminder of the adventure she'd hoped to have. Or at least an experience she wouldn't have back in Portugal. The future stepping in when she was in danger of forgetting what they were now. Forgetting that it was never going back to the way things were with silly playfulness. Forgetting that, according to him, things had never been that way to begin with.

In danger of falling under the spell of old desires, the hope that things could turn around with them. Every time they shared a smile, it punched through her defenses, even punched through her exceedingly legitimate anger at him. Weakened her.

He obviously felt it, too, the wall she'd reconstructed, as he took a final bite and stood up before he'd even swallowed it. But before he went to return the tray, he stopped to say, "You should go see them, but come back and finish dinner after."

Still on about her eating after he'd done his best to wipe her appetite from existence.

As she stared at the tiny words on her screen, her desire to do the responsible thing wavered for once. She wanted to see the sky.

When she didn't respond to his nag to eat, West took his tray and left, grumbling beneath his breath as he went. Something else new about the bearded man, or just another fissure in the usually perfectly polished appearance and persona of the man she'd known. And she wouldn't let that feel like progress with him, even if she would have months ago when that had been her primary aim: get closer without driving the man who never spoke of his past away for badgering him about his past. Fat lot of good that had done.

If she just popped out for a minute, she could see the sky, and then come back inside, answer the most urgent emails before the satellite moved out of range and get the rest loaded to send the next temporary internet zone in twelve hours. She hadn't looked at the four emails that had popped up, but had looked long enough to confirm that none of them were from her father, then went about finishing the first one she'd started.

Hoping her father would answer her after all this time was probably another reason she was stupid. She'd been sending weekly emails to entreat him to contact her, reassure him things were fine, not putting any pressure to bear on him to explain himself, but still no word. It didn't really surprise her. She wished it did.

As she worked on the one email, a mass exodus of the galley happened. The people who'd been there all summer with daylight skies and no canvas for the aurora australis might not get another chance. They didn't start and stop with the flip of a switch, and the skies trended toward twilight now, with darkness far out into the wide, flat, fairly creepy distance—so different from her mountainous Douro River homeland.

As soon as she hit Send, she zipped into the light indoor jacket she wore all the time, returned her tray and hurried outside. Everyone's hurry to get out there had informed her decision not to go back to her cabin for warmer attire. She'd be fine for a quick pop out, and if she got too cold, she'd visit the saunas she'd only discovered yesterday.

When she finally made it outside, she found herself at the back of a crowd, all heads turned toward the flat horizon.

She stepped to one side and another, weaseling her way to a spot where she could best view the looming dark.

"You didn't miss it," West said from beside her, her first indication he was nearby.

"Did you make it out in time to see some?"

"I wasn't bent over my mobile phone." He smiled a little.

So there had been some, but he felt confident there would be more?

She tugged her ever-present hat down more firmly on

her ears and shoved her hands into her pockets. "How do you know they'll recur?"

He turned back to the horizon. She actually felt him look away from her, because she'd determined not to watch him. She'd also determined not to interact much, and yet... here she was, interacting.

"I'm only staying a bit. It's too cold to watch nothing happening except the approaching dark, which is neat in a different way."

"It is," he agreed, then added, "Usually when aurora happen, they happen for a little while. It's not a one-off. Comes in waves."

"You've seen them before?"

"Not here. In Scotland. Years ago."

Something else she hadn't known about him. His accent and name gave away his homeland, but she'd not known he'd been far enough north to view the aurora borealis.

"On holiday or at home?"

As privileged an upbringing as she'd had, with money and travel, Lia had never traveled north far enough to see the northern lights. When she skied, she went to the Alps. The rest of the time, she went to warmer places.

"Where I lived."

Where he'd lived...not at home?

"Where was that?" she asked, unable to stop herself.

"Hmm?" He glanced sideways at her, and she was watching him again, not the sky. "Inverness, mostly. Kinlochleven for a while."

"Where's that?"

"North." He looked back at the sky, then touched her insulated arm. "You want to haver on about nothin' important, or see the aurora?"

A murmur rose from the crowd just after his words, drawing her gaze back to the horizon, which now glowed

a strange, unearthly green in a general, diffuse and…
disappointing manner.

Not the light show she'd expected.

She'd watched videos in preparation for her trip, doc-
umentaries. She'd looked at photos and read blogs about
viewing the aurora australis.

"Is that it?" she asked, truly beginning to feel the cold.
Excitement had kept it a background buzzing before that,
but a bit of green sky in the far distance?

"Might repeat like that. Dunno." He frowned as she
pulled her hands from the thin pockets and began rubbing
them together, then stuffed them back into the pockets in
the vain hope of not contracting some dreaded Frozen Antarctic Finger syndrome. Or frostbite. That one was a real
thing. "But if it is, you'll have plenty of time to see them
again, catalog the colors and whatever, over the winter. If
you're stayin'."

"I'm staying," she repeated. The man wasn't going to
stop poking her to go. Until he went. When the lot of them
were finally forever gone.

Ugh, she was wasting her time.

More important things to do than watch a whole lot of
nothing spectacular happen. "I'm going in."

"Give it another minute," West said, and it should've
sounded like an order, but the softness of his voice was all
velvet suggestion, coaxing.

Two more days until the transport bus began driving
people the short distance to the coast where boats waited
to spirit them back to the world. Two days and then she
wouldn't see him anymore. Maybe never again after.

It was more that thought than anything that had her
pausing, looking back to the sky.

People kept shifting and blocking her view, so she edged
into West's space to see the horizon.

The glow was there, rippling a bit or pulsing. She wasn't

sure what to call it. Not something to fill her with wonder, as she'd hoped. But just when disappointment began to settle over her, the green grew brighter, and then rippled out, glowing fingers reaching from the dark horizon toward the twilight sky under which they stood.

It moved slowly at first, and then faster in undulating waves that almost looked alive.

She wasn't aware of having made any decisions, just the cold all around her, the dancing sky above her and one warmer hand. Because she'd grabbed his.

Not breathing. The murmuring that had taken hold of the crowd faded to reverent silence. All around them, the wind that continuously blew across the barren landscape whispered and whistled. Her own ragged breathing brought something low and deep into it, and the rapid beat of her heart. The music of a desolate, majestic landscape. Life and beauty where there should be none, deepened by the large, strong hand in her own.

The hand he wouldn't want to be holding.

Because this was something *she* felt. Not him. Not for her. Never for her.

It didn't take long for the truth of her situation to come swimming back to her mind, and with it, she found the strength and self-respect to unfold her fingers from his.

Under the glow of the green and yellow aurora, she felt his gaze on her instead of the sky, and balled her hands at her sides to keep from performing another round of self-destructive stupid.

One-two-three-four-five-six-seven-eight-nine-ten.

She counted heartbeats pounding so fast that she wouldn't have been able to breathe at all had she been saying the numbers aloud. Too fast. Too hard.

She closed her eyes.

Go in.

Go back in and take care of what was expected of her. Emails. Work. Sleep. Repeat.

She hadn't started moving—the thoughts had appeared in her mind, chiding her, shaming her into action—when she felt West's hand enfold her tight, cold fist again.

He didn't stop there, just gave a little tug until she was standing in front of him, and then repeated with her other hand, wrapping both in warmth.

"West?"

"You're cold," he said softly over her shoulder, holding her hands and keeping close, but somehow managing not to put his arms fully around her to do it.

She *was* cold. She should wish to be colder on the inside, to grow a callus around her still-smarting heart, to be as cold inside as she was outside. If it would help, she'd strip herself bare and pack her body in the snow like a kid packed himself in sand at the beach.

Coldhearted, less prone to emotion, more to reason. Then she could reason her way through how stupid it was to let him warm her hands when it also warmed her heart and a hollow she'd been babying for months.

The forking fingers of the green light show in the sky retreated, and even if the next round was guaranteed to be more spectacular than that, she'd still have gone inside. It was too confusing with West, and while she'd pretended she was only angry until she'd seen him, since then the wound had been ripped fresh open. It had never closed, never had the chance to scar. And if she knew anything about wounds and scarring, she knew the scar got thicker, grizzlier and harder to ignore the more times it was re-opened.

A few words said, and she extracted her hands from his to put some distance between them, and hurried inside to her emails and responsibilities.

Two days couldn't come fast enough.

CHAPTER SIX

ALTHOUGH TONY BRADSHAW had taken them to winter hours only a couple days prior, after a day of nonstop injuries while maintenance crews worked to prepare the station to overwinter he had decided to keep the clinic and hospital open for a second shift. And, because he'd felt ill, had asked Lia to stay on and pull a double shift.

She'd said yes—not just because he was ill, but because it kept her busy and not obsessing over the final email that had arrived last night while she was holding hands with Weston MacIntyre under the aurora. The one that said her father had turned up at a Barcelona hospital. The one she hadn't seen or responded to until there was no signal, leaving her to only queue it up for the next moment her device could catch some bandwidth.

"All right, Mr. Hansen," she said to the man who'd most recently entered, wheeling the breathing machine into one treatment area and getting the liquid medicine dispensed into the breathing apparatus. "Have you done this before?"

He nodded, his breathing still labored. "More…and… more…frequently." He breathed shallow and fast, his speech broken as she started the vaporizer and held it over his mouth.

"In deep. If you can, try to tuck your tongue to the side or press to the roof of your mouth and breathe around it.

This stuff is dreadfully bitter, but it works like magic on swollen airways."

He took over holding the mouthpiece, and she watched as, over no more than half a minute, his breathing became deeper, less labored.

Mr. Hansen wasn't a complicated patient, so she might even be able to pop out and get some dinner to bring back and eat here once he was hooked up.

The station had gone into some kind of carnival atmosphere, a party in the galley with nonstop food rolling, drinks and music. There were two bars at the station that had their own farewell parties going. The coffeehouse was full of folk music and desserts, or so she'd heard. Made sense. Buffet your way through dinner, then finish up in the coffeehouse with cake and pastries. Not her, she couldn't be gone that long, but the galley wasn't terribly far way.

And West would probably be there.

Okay, maybe she wouldn't go. Although, with twenty minutes before her emails might finally get a response, a trip might keep her from obsessing and worrying about the email that had arrived while she was outside, holding hands with West under the aurora.

Her father had turned up in a hospital in Barcelona.

Hospital.

Now she couldn't stop herself running through possible scenarios to turn him up in a hospital. Accidents. Illnesses. Things just bad enough that a normal person would seek the comfort of family over… Then she felt guilty for almost hoping his hospital visit was serious enough to make him reach out, while still being recoverable.

Hansen didn't need her. The crews must also be on dinner break, or they were all injured and the work was no longer getting done, because her steady supply of distractions just dried up in the eleventh hour.

She went to tell him she was going to dash to the gal-ley, when a man's alarmed voice sounded from the entry, and got her moving that direction.

Two men carried a woman who had a massive slice open down the side of her calf. They tried to hold a com-press and stop the bleeding as they carried her, but it still dripped rapidly enough to switch off every other thought in her head.

"In here." Lia flipped on the lights in the trauma room, and they carried in her patient, placing her on the table while Lia washed her hands and shoved them into gloves. "Someone tell me what happened."

"Fan blade," one man said. "Came off. We were trying to fix one of the in-loaders."

In-loader? No clue. But fan-blade accident made sense. She grabbed several packets of gauze pads, ripped them open and wheeled them on a tray with other implements toward the woman. "What's your name?"

"Gossen," her patient said, pale around the mouth, her brows a deep, angry red that could've been from crying, or just the ferocity with which her brows crammed together. "Eileen Gossen."

"Okay, Eileen. I'm going to need to look at this." She took over holding the compress. "I want you to lie back and relax as much as you can. The harder your heart beats, the more blood pumps, the more comes out the wound, okay? Lie back."

She didn't take time to warn, just grabbed the fresh compresses, and got a quick peek at the wound as she switched them out. Not spurting. But deep. "Do you want me to tell you what I saw, or do you just want me to fix it?"

"Both," Eileen said, voice strained.

"All right. The blade hit veins, that's why you're bleed-ing so freely. It did not hit an artery—there was no spurt-ing. That's good news." She pointed to the one man who'd continued lingering after the other who'd helped carry in Eileen had left. "I need some help. I want you to go to the galley and look for either Dr. Flynn or Dr. MacIntyre. MacIntyre will probably be easiest to find—he's the tall, broad-shouldered Scot with the black beard. Always wears a navy knit cap."

"You can't do it alone?" Eileen asked, sounding more worried that she needed backup.

"I'm a trained surgeon, Eileen. I can stitch this up so beautifully that, in a couple years, people will have a hard time believing you were ever injured. But I don't want to remove my hands from where I'm placing pressure in order to do the other things I want done to make sure you're as well taken care of as possible."

"What things?"

"Monitoring your blood pressure. Setting an IV and getting saline hung just in case you've lost more blood than I can see from this. I don't want you losing more while I try to make sure you didn't lose too much. Okay?"

Eileen nodded, and when Lia looked back to the man, he was already gone. She should've asked if he even knew Jordan or West. If worse came to worst, she could call for Tony. The medical director's cabin abutted the clinic, but with the way that man had shuffled around and slurred his speech, she didn't want to take a chance on him. It might even be better to go for it alone if Jordan or West failed to materialize. Was this how things would be over the winter? She might have to do a survey of all who remained behind and see if there was any medical training at all among them. CPR, firefighting, anything. Or make some learn. For emergency situations. Something about Tony's manner tonight unsettled her.

But she didn't have time for that. She needed to keep Eileen calm, so Lia kept talking. Asking questions. Where was she from? What was her job in the station? Was this her first tour in Antarctica?

It didn't take long for the man to fetch West, but her gentle, friendly, nonemergency questions helped Eileen relax. Her breathing leveled out. Her pulse, which Lia kept monitoring with one hand on the woman's ankle while she maintained pressure with the other, had slowed.

"What've we got?" West asked before his feet even crossed the threshold into the trauma room.

"This is Eileen. She has an overachieving slice on the right side of her right calf, and it's bleeding freely. Can you get a cuff on her and then a line in? We're also going to need anesthetic—that's the third thing."

"BP. IV. Anesthetic. Can do."

She kept pressure on until he'd given her a BP reading that let her know her blood loss wasn't yet to threatening levels, but that didn't mean she was going to change her mind on the IV.

"Do you want me to hang saline?" he asked, setting and flushing the line to make sure it was clear before taping it down.

"Yes." Lia and West never really worked together in a trauma situation. She'd assisted him in surgeries when her fellowship surgeries got light and he was in regular rotation as a general surgeon at their hospital, but they'd been more the usual surgeries than something dialed to emergency levels.

They fell into a kind of unspoken coordination. He monitored everything—blood pressure, pain management, the patient's emotional state—and she cleaned the wound and stitched, starting with the nicked vein, then moving on up. Eileen was lucky—the cut was remarkably clean. Fan blade sounded scary, but did less damage than she'd seen in some knife-wound repairs. Or, God help anyone, what

bullets did once they entered the body and began weap-
onizing bone fragments.

In the middle of all that, she heard her phone go off,
but had to ignore it. And not hurry just because she didn't
want to miss the window, even though missing the window would mean she'd have another twenty-four hours to
sweat out a response.

By the time it was over and she'd bandaged everything,
Eileen had actually dozed off from the pain medication.

"We should move her into one of the patient beds," she
said to West. "And let her sleep it off."

Her phone chirped again and she winced. "Actually,
can you just put the railing up on her bed and let her sleep
here for a few minutes while I go? I have to get this. I've
been waiting for an email—kind of an emergency, too."

"Emergency at home?" West asked, doing as she asked
and putting the rail up before following her out.

"Yeah…" she answered, then flipped on her phone. The
three-word subject line hit like a truck.

Vitor Monterrosa located

"If you can, maybe peek in on Tony? He's… He's un-
well. But only if Eileen is well and truly out. I'll hurry. I
just… I…"

"Go."

She flew out of the clinic and off to a corner of a nearby
lounge to pore over news from home.

West watched the doorway long after Lia had gone. It
shouldn't have made him feel good that she'd sent for him
when she'd needed help, and he hated that it did.

The tension in her forehead when she'd asked him to
stay had done a lot to undo that good feeling. The news
that Tony was sick enough to call off had burned through

the rest of it. If his health was going the way it seemed the past few weeks, she'd effectively be locking herself into a dangerous winter prison for eight months without access to any other doctors. Not a fan. Not for her.

Her hands had twitched when her phone pinged, telling him everything he needed to know about how serious the emergency was. Twitching hands were a big deal for surgeons, and she was usually steady enough he'd trust her with the life of anyone—family, if he'd had any left. As steady and predictable as his inability to be there for the people who needed him.

He hovered in the door of the trauma room with one eye trained on Eileen and the rest of his attention split between the short hallway to Tony's quarters, and the main lobby doors for Lia's return, or the arrival of more patients.

Eileen woke shortly and he had things to do, a legitimate, healthy way to clear his mind of the worry and guilt snapping at his heels, but not long enough. It took practically no time to transfer her to one of the four patient beds in the hospital ward, explain everything, ask a couple of questions and give a much longer-lasting shot for pain management.

When he was done, and Lia still hadn't returned, he broke off to seek out Tony.

He wanted to be flip about how *emergency* it could be, just to steady his own nerves. From all of Lia's descriptions, there was so much quaint and peaceful about the medieval walled village attached to her family's ancestral estate it was hard to even picture any real, modern emergencies there—whether it was *a mess*, as she'd recently stated, or not.

Fire and acts of God seemed like the extent of what could happen. But believing that would mean believing she was overreacting now, and that seemed less likely.

He knocked upon reaching Tony's door. Checking on

the medical director was one thing he could quickly do to help Lia and occupy himself.

What he saw when the door opened did nothing to soothe his worry.

Sweat dripped off the man, as if he'd just run a marathon at the equator. His hair stuck up in all directions, except for the pieces around his face, which stuck to his forehead and overly defined cheekbones. Most disconcerting was how pale he was, even in that obviously sweaty, overheated condition.

"I was going to ask if you were all right, but I see you're not," West said, instead of greeting him. "I'll be right back. I need some tools."

"I just picked up a bug," Tony called behind him, words meant as a weak argument, but West didn't stop until he'd retrieved the nurse on a stick, a stethoscope, and pulled up his new patient's record on his device.

He didn't even bother knocking when he had returned, just let himself in as if it were a patient's room.

He'd actually been after Tony about increasing his caloric intake for about a month, but not doggedly enough. The man was a physician; he knew symptoms when they were plaguing him, one would think.

"If this is a bug, you have an immune system problem."

"I don't."

"You've had a few bugs lately, then?"

"Lia complaining?"

"No. Worried. She's like that." West wasn't there to fight; he was there to help, and would force his help on Tony whether he wanted it or not.

"You two knew each other before, right?"

"Yes. But that's not what we're talking about."

"I've noticed tension between the two of you. Everyone has."

West folded his arms. "If you're overwintering, you

need to be checked now. Blood work, vitals. I respect you, I don't want to be a jerk, but I wouldn't be doing my job if I didn't force the issue when you clearly need help."

That earned him a wince. With the way Tony had been fighting all mentions of whatever was going on with him, West had a feeling he already knew something serious and was doing his best to ignore it. Not a great feeling to start an examination with.

"I understand not wanting to think about bad things, but sometimes you have to. Sometimes it's the best option. So, sit here and I'll get vitals and some blood. Start simple, do a CBC. If you've got an infection, it'll show. Then we can go from there."

When he turned to fetch the phlebotomy tray, Tony said quietly, "I have some swollen lymph nodes."

West looked back to see the man gesturing at his collarbone.

In his head, he went spinning through the symptoms he'd been mentally cataloging. Swollen lymph nodes alone could be anything, usually something that would resolve on its own, but when combined with the fatigue, weight loss and night sweats... Not a great string of symptoms.

"Anything else?" he asked.

Tony listed a couple more and increased West's alarm.

"I'll grab the ultrasound, too," West said, but asked first, "Are they sore?"

"No."

"Movable?"

"I don't know..." Tony said, but his tone said he did.

It was never comfortable for colleagues to examine one another, but when the possible diagnosis was such a dire one... West left the door open and went to check on the suspicious nodes indicated, but found two other smaller, unmovable nodes around Tony's clavicle.

Fixed. Hard. Not sore.

Damn.

"I'll get the cart."

"Tell me," Tony said, interrupting his flight.

West was a surgeon by specialty. He didn't usually diagnose cancer—he was the guy who cut it out once another doctor had these awful conversations.

"One of medium size and two smaller ones under the jaw." West explained what he'd felt. "Let me get the card."

Tony knew those symptoms; they could be benign, but when unmovable, hard lymph nodes got involved...

Once in the lobby, he paused long enough to check that Eileen was still asleep, then scribbled *Bradshaw* on a note for Lia, and headed back.

Still not back. And he didn't have time to think on it, or go find her.

A quick scan confirmed the solidity of the nodes, and added a fourth deeper one he hadn't felt before. The likelihood that this was benign plummeted.

"You think lymphoma?" Tony said the question with an astonishingly calm tone.

Stress made these things worse, and West didn't want to lay that extra weight on him. Didn't want to have this conversation, like so many bad conversations, especially when he couldn't say for certain without a biopsy. "I'm worried. It needs more than we can provide here."

Sweat continued rolling off Tony, but the calm persisted. "If it is, I won't be able to stay."

"Sorry, man. I'll run these labs now. You take some acetaminophen to try and lower the fever."

West returned to the lobby and found a red-eyed Lia leaving Eileen's room. The second time he'd ever seen her actively crying, and was starting to realize she could never hide it.

"What happened?" he asked immediately, wheeling the ultrasound to the side of the room and grabbing the blood samples in one hand and Lia's hand in the other to pull her into the lab with him. "Something with the vineyard?"

"O pai," she answered in Portuguese, her voice thick and froggy—something he liked in bed, but not like this. "He was in the hospital in Barcelona. But he's not now. Why did you need the ultrasound?"

"Tony." He answered that first, but moved back to the subject of her father. A hospital visit didn't sound worthy of tears, unless the outcome had been bad. "Is your father all right?"

Her slender shoulders crept up. "I don't know. I guess. He's been gone so long. The only time we get a lead on him is when he pops up to withdraw money at a bank, right before he immediately leaves that city. They emailed to say that they thought he was in Spain, and then they needed family to contact them, and by the time the email came, it was too late."

Family emergency. Nothing to do with the anachronistic village that had no motor vehicles inside the wall.

One emergency at a time. He got the CBC started while she explained.

The idea that her father had stayed gone didn't make sense to him, especially knowing what a chauvinist the man was—not leaving the vineyard to her. It also made it seem a little more reasonable that as soon as she found out where one of them was, she'd gone. He didn't sigh, wouldn't sigh, or walk out on another important conversation with her. Sometimes you had to talk about bad things. When there were no other options.

"What was he admitted for?"

"Observation." She croaked the word, focusing on him like he'd have an answer, or anything that could ease her worry. "But they wouldn't say more, except to tell me where he was staying. I rang the investigator, who's still in Barcelona, and sent him there, then waited for a response, but my father was already gone. Checked out this morning. Yesterday morning? Tomorrow? Time zones. Whatever. He was gone and…" She finished her statement with a helpless shrug.

"It doesn't sound like he wants to be found, love."

Her bitter, incredulous laughing shrug shamed him. She might as well have said, *How does this keep happening to me?*

"The whole point to finding him is to know he's all right, and to tell him not to worry about the vineyard. My tour here will be over two months before reconstruction is projected to finish. I'll be staying there forever. The welfare of the village or the people there who rely on Monterrosa Wine is no longer on him, and he truly never wanted it to be passed to him to start with. He doesn't have to keep running. Just let me know he's okay. But now? Under observation? That could be for anything. Injury. Illness. Am I supposed to just stop looking?"

All the things she said, when broken apart into singular elements, didn't add up to alarming. But with his own history of having an addict brother, it did. It definitely did.

"No," he said immediately, and then, "Lia, I know you don't want to hear this. I know I sound like a stuck recording, but you should go home. Having this time lag between sent and received communication isn't helping. Listen to me. I'll stay. I'll take the winter. Tony is leaving. He's…"

"What was the ultrasound for?"

"Looks like lymphoma. He has to go home for a biopsy at the least, and probably treatment. So they're going to have to get another doctor down here for that NASA project. You're going to be on your own for a while, maybe a couple of weeks until they get someone else. Say the word, and I'll take your spot. If your father is in trouble and you're here, you'll hate yourself if something worse happens. I know what I'm talking about."

She stilled, her damp eyes growing sharper beneath a pinched brow as she searched his face. "Did something happen to Charlie?"

Damn it. He really sucked at keeping secrets suddenly. She was in pain and he needed to help, so he just blurted things out.

"Yes," he answered quietly, because he couldn't see a way out of it. "Life is short, sometimes people need help holding on to it for a while longer. You don't get past that kind of failing."

"But you never said…"

"No reason to."

She stilled, her brows screwed to incredulity for several seconds, and he could see her doing the mental calculations. She knew. She might not know the details, but the sudden compassion on her face said she knew that Charlie's death was the thing that had happened while she was gone.

"West…" She breathed his name, and as soon as his hands were free of the computer interface to get the CBC started, she took his nearest hand in both of hers. "I'm so sorry. And I'm sorry I wasn't there. What happened?"

"I don't want to talk about it with you." The words came in a rush. She couldn't be the one offering comfort. His trauma was in the past, hers was here now, currently mid-death spiral. He pulled his hand free.

The retreat did the trick, and she stepped fully back from him, but the sympathy and concern he saw written plainly on her face didn't budge, even when she nodded, and she softly said, "Okay. I'll…just… Thank you for your help with Eileen."

She was leaving. And he'd left their conversation on a note that would keep her from hearing what he'd said. After today, he wouldn't have any more chances to help her through this.

"Wait." He set the second vial of blood in the caddy of the next machine, and followed her. "Lia."

"I need to check on Eileen."

Not allowing her to dismiss him, he waited in the lobby for her return, letting her have a moment to catch her breath without him crowding the air. But the second she stepped back out of Eileen's room, he asked, "Your father...did he deliberately start the fire?"

He saw her shutters coming down as she looked at him for a long, heavy moment, trying to decide if she was going to answer. He'd just told her he didn't want to talk to her about Charlie, but here he was, digging into her own personal business.

She handled it with far more grace than he had. "I don't think he did it on purpose. My father didn't want me to inherit the vineyard, but he didn't want to run it, either. He had these great dreams about having a son to pass it on to, and didn't manage to pull that off before retirement age, even with three wives."

She watched him cautiously as she answered, telling him more about her life at every turn now than when they'd been together. Even than when they'd been planning the wedding. He'd guarded information about his past, and done everything he could to keep her eyes on the horizon, and where they were going, not where they'd come from. And now that he wasn't trying to keep from having to repay her information with his own, he let her speak. He wanted her to speak.

"He wouldn't burn it down rather than give it to you?"

"I don't think he hates me..." she said, but it didn't sound like she was sure. He had to remind himself that this was the man whose disappearance still caused her tears. "If he'd done it on purpose, he wouldn't have run. Running from *failure* is more like my father than running from guilt."

"How do you set a whole lot of land and a castle on fire by accident if there are no other problems exacerbating the situation?"

"It's not a castle," she argued, then sighed. "But if he was drinking, that doesn't mean—"

"It doesn't mean he did it on purpose, it doesn't mean he's a drunk," West filled in. "But it might mean there is a bigger problem than simply 'my father doesn't want to run the vineyard anymore.'"

"He's not an alcoholic," she reiterated, one hand waving, her head about to shake off her shoulders. "You have a travel day tomorrow. Go. Get some sleep. Thank you for your help."

Still trying to dismiss him, and still upset.

He should go, just as she suggested, but he couldn't ever sleep through alarm bells. And there was Tony Bradshaw still to deal with, but he didn't want to leave it on that note. Especially when one of them would definitely be leaving for real in the morning.

"I could stay and let you get some rest—you're taking over the station tomorrow." Pathetic offer, which he knew she wouldn't accept any more than she was yet willing to accept his offer to winter in her place.

"I probably slept more last night than you did."

"Did I keep you awake?"

"You can't sniff without me hearing it."

But that would all end tomorrow, and the simple thought churned his stomach. "At least I didn't prowl the corridor like a lion."

She didn't even try to smile until he'd mimed her snarl and slow-witted claw swipe of the air, then she managed a little one.

"I'd best go sleep, then," he said, but his feet didn't move. He couldn't look away from her. Looked too long, too hard, too fraught…

"What?" She gave another little sad sniff that pushed him over the edge.

Without letting himself think it through, West grabbed her by the back of the neck and hauled her against his chest, wrapping his arms tight about her.

She didn't fight him an ounce, just buried her face in the crook of his neck and snaked her arms around his waist, then leaned.

He'd wanted to comfort her, but with her pressed to him, her breath fanning the side of his neck, the chaos of the station, of the world, seemed to fade away. It wasn't relief, though it was something like that. It wasn't lust, but that was always there, too, when he touched her, when he even looked at her. He just felt better, touching her. Like hope was a thing that could still exist.

He could feel her fists balling in the back of his shirts, a light tremble shaking her whole body. But she wasn't going to let him save her, even if she clung on to him for dear life. That steel spine he loved was still there even if it was occasionally washed by tears. Still fighting for people she loved. Even when they repeatedly let her down.

He squeezed a little tighter, dipped his head to breathe her in and suddenly realized the low-level headache he'd been nursing for months was gone, and it had left a strange kind of euphoria in its wake.

"If you change your mind, say the word. I'll stay." He whispered the words into her ear, and although it could've only been taken as a repeat of the offer he'd made to let her go home, that wasn't even what he'd meant. And that was exactly what he'd been afraid of: reaching that point where he would abandon his plans and principles to be with her. If she didn't keep pushing him away, the entire drive that had him telling her ugly lies.

She nodded; he already knew she wouldn't say the words. And he was lucky she wouldn't.

He'd be leaving tomorrow, and that would be the end of it. He'd go wherever the hell he was going to go, take the first connecting flight out of Dallas to parts unknown and be forced to email her daily to check in, make sure another doctor had arrived, that she was okay…

Not a clean break.

Maybe there never could be a clean break with her. She didn't know how to give up on people she loved. Even when they really didn't deserve her compassion.

He held her until she relaxed enough for the trembling to stop, and she was the one to pull away. He would've kept holding her, even standing there, in the middle of the clinic.

"Go to sleep," she croaked, but added sincerely and re-signedly, "Thank you for all your help tonight. Safe travels. I hope you find what you're looking for."

Not just good night, but goodbye. This goodbye was a true goodbye, and he heard it for what it was this time. Not a Charlie goodbye—she wasn't going to push poison into her veins when he left—but a goodbye he still might never get over. She'd never track him down again, or maybe even email. Probably wouldn't have asked for his help at all to-night if she'd had other options.

He'd pushed, and she'd backed off, as soon as she un-derstood. Or as soon as she'd accepted the lie he'd told her. She might have just shared one hell of an emotional load with him, but she didn't expect anything from him. This time was real, and he felt the difference in his marrow.

And in his empty, aching arms as he walked away.

CHAPTER SEVEN

"YOU'RE GOING TO make it on time," Lia reassured the station's bus driver, pressing the mouthpiece of the nebulizer back to her mouth. "Panicking about delaying your departure schedule isn't helping. They can't leave without you. You're the driver."

"But...so...many...trips...today."

"I know." Lia parsed out the meaning of the broken speech, having grown more used to the breathless cadence of an asthma attack since she'd arrived. It was amazing how subzero air triggered them in people, even those who may have never had any signs of asthma in the past. She'd gone into the system this morning to order another crate of the vaporizing liquid to arrive before shipping stopped. Just to be prepared. Running out over the winter sounded like a deadly situation.

Another ten minutes and she'd go with Kasey, the driver, out to the bus to say goodbye to Jordan and Zeke, who were in the first departure slot this morning. She didn't know when West was scheduled, or Tony, whom she'd be glad to see go for the good of his health. She'd forced a couple nutrient-dense drinks on him this morning after having finished the labs West started last night. She just knew there was one trip scheduled every other hour today, and that by the time the trips resumed tomorrow, two-thirds of the station would already be gone.

"The deeper you breathe, the faster it vaporizes and the sooner you'll be on your way."

Luck was with her. When Kasey had finished her treatment and Lia had given her an injection of steroids and an emergency inhaler, they both bundled into their coats and hurried out of the station.

Almost as soon as she stepped outside, Lia regretted not having made time to say goodbye to Jordan earlier. It wasn't blowing hard, but snow fell heavily, and after how much she avoided the outdoors here, it was the first time she'd actually seen it coming down since she'd arrived. Big, fat, fluffy flakes drifted down from the heavens, painting the world ethereal shades of bluish white. The bus wasn't far, and was still somewhat visible. Would the heavy snowfall make driving more difficult here? Did it stop having all meaning when everything was covered by more than a mile-thick snow and pack ice? One more thing to worry about.

When they reached the boarding side, Lia made out three figures waiting.

Not just Jordan and Zeke—West stood to the side, a few feet away, making clear that he wasn't there with them. He was just among those waiting for her.

Kasey hurried onto the bus after a sharp word about dawdling, and Jordan and Zeke launched in immediately with farewells, promises to call, hugs, kisses on her cold cheeks and an oath to send more tea lights for her heater.

She barely heard any of it. The words may have made it to her brain, but they drifted away almost immediately, her attention so divided by the idea that West had waited to say goodbye this time. Even after he'd hugged her last night, she hadn't expected it. She also realized in that moment that she hadn't been letting herself think about him being gone, not for a couple of days. Especially not since last night, when she'd needed him.

She'd come to say goodbye, never thinking that she'd have to say it twice. That having it out with him and then spending more than a week around one another would allow the old familiarity to build back up. That she might even get to know him better after she'd given him back their engagement ring.

If she asked, he would take her place and stay the winter, he'd said.

If she asked, would he take Tony's? How much harder would it be to say goodbye for a third time once winter was over?

Jordan and Zeke pulled away and West met her gaze again. A cold couple of feet and a miles-wide canyon separated them. In the freeze, his naturally pale cheeks had turned pink, and bits of fluff clung to the navy knit cap he wore. Even looking so different as when he was temporarily hers, when she met his gaze her heart gave one sluggish thud and then began to rabbit away inside her chest.

It was quiet; the falling snow deafened the sound. She heard her own breathing but nothing else.

The bus ran at his back; she saw the exhaust fogging the air, Kasey no doubt going through the checks to get it going, but maybe also waiting for them to finish up. Not that they'd even started.

It was just heavy eye contact, and pensive frowns, no words. No actual goodbyes were uttered. It was like the slow-motion repeat of her first day in the station, but when he looked at her, she didn't see anger. Just sadness. Resignation. Worry. Because even if he didn't love her, had never loved her, he still cared enough to be worried. And last night she'd given him plenty to worry about. But then, he'd done the same for her. She knew he wasn't okay, the loss of his only family couldn't let him be okay, but he didn't want her involved. So it hung in the frosty air, both of them so much more aware now of the battles going on in the background, and letting the fight continue, unaided. He'd been right in not marrying her. Not in leaving the way he had, but that he couldn't marry her.

She still didn't know what to say.

He pulled his bare hands from his pockets and reached out to take her left hand. She hadn't had time to grab the big coat, or get on gloves. Her fingers, cold to the point of stiffness, still slid into his in a pattern that couldn't be familiar. He'd never been a handholder. Probably something else that should've alarmed her, back when they were trying to build their own forever. Probably something she shouldn't have shrugged off, or explained away.

Now, the heat of his hand thawed hers, his thumb stroking the well-worn rut that still existed where his ring once sat. The ring she'd spied on the chain around his neck, once and then not again.

Kasey gave the motor a rev—she heard that—and cracked the door to shout for West to get on if he was coming.

Still no words from him, or her. He just looked back at her again, a long, heavy look she might forever link with quietly falling snow and skies like twilight. The summer was gone, and autumn twilight would soon turn to winter night. It felt appropriate, like the end of everything.

Releasing her hand, he stepped forward, pushed the brim of her hat up to expose her forehead and leaned in to kiss her head. Warm whiskered tenderness.

She was going to miss him. Even if he wasn't hers anymore.

Before he got away, she flung her arms around his shoulders and hugged as hard as she could through the layers of insulated suits, and pressed her mouth to his ear to whisper the only words that came. Words for herself, an acknowledgment of what she'd lost, in her native tongue, and what it did to her. Safe words. Words she could only say because he'd never understand.

He looked confused as she stepped back, but she didn't stay to explain herself, just turned to hurry inside. She didn't need to watch them leave. Waving felt like an act of cheer, not bitter resignation.

Besides, she had a job to do. Even if people were being trucked away en masse from the station for the next couple of days, she still had a significant number of people to worry after right now. Now was all she could focus on.

Somewhere warmer.

Inside.

Away from the starkness of bluish-white.

The rest of Lia's day creaked by. Yesterday's onslaught of injuries had subsided, and she was left with a few small incidents and Eileen, who was now reconsidering her winter plans. She'd be on crutches for a couple weeks to minimize the stress to her leg, and that felt like being completely useless to someone whose job description included climbing into the ducts and other small spaces to fix things.

By the end of the day, the station felt like a ghost town, and Lia still carried with her the starkness of bluish-white.

Tomorrow, the numbers would shrink by another couple hundred, with all summer personnel gone aside from the extended janitorial staff who still had work to do, cleaning parts of the station that would go unused for the winter and be closed off to conserve power and the fuel needed to generate it. Another reason she was so thankful for the little tea-light heater West had given her. She could be warm without further depleting the fuel.

Tomorrow, after it had been cleaned, she'd move into Tony's cabin. She didn't want to move into someone else's space—it felt like moving into a stranger's home—but it came with the job. It wasn't unlike taking care of her village at home, only here it was the health of dozens, and at home it was the welfare of hundreds. Still, it felt kind of like practice. A case study in how to mingle living and working together.

Only at home, she wouldn't be expected to carry a radio with her at all times. Being on call twenty-four hours a day, and praying there were no genuine emergencies. She was a surgeon, and a good one—no one with mediocre surgical skills could get a neurosurgery fellowship—but since she'd returned home, she'd had to admit to herself that she was suited to a smaller GP practice, as well. Building a relationship with patients from cradle to grave appealed in some way that felt more meaningful than the prestige and excitement of neurosurgery. Something she could only admit to herself in hindsight, when the idea of performing emergency surgery by herself here, without any experienced medical personnel to assist, was enough to make her want to stow away on one of the boats back to civilization.

But that move would wait until tomorrow. She had the radio with her, the volume cranked up to levels she'd never have dared to use if there were other people sleeping nearby, and that would suffice for tonight.

Not ready to go sleep in another man's bed. May never be fully ready, even if she might one day make that decision—once she knew if her father's will was ironclad or not. She hadn't told West that he'd almost inherited a vineyard by marrying her—it only remained hers while she was unmarried. She hadn't known it until he was already gone. And even if she would've trusted him with the vineyard, she wasn't sure she could picture giving that power to anyone else. She didn't even want people finding out and it suddenly becoming a thing to try and woo her in order to inherit a vineyard. Pai should've thought of these things before that silly bit of legal tomfoolery.

This time away was supposed to be about adventure, but it might just be about mourning. Repairing herself.

West's cabin was empty, as was the rest of Pod C, which would be soon shuttered for the winter like other empty parts of the station. After ten days of thin walls and hearing every little thing, she was now the only one there, surrounded by empty rooms and the loudest silence.

She could sleep in his room tonight if she wanted to, maybe move to one of the warmer cabins. Or maybe just dart in and pinch his pillow to keep the essence of him around for a while.

Like she'd kept his ring on her finger last time.

The thought effectively killed her pathetic, sentimental urges. An instant ice bath to her dignity.

She set up the heater, lit the candles, lifted the blinds on her window, then wrestled her feet out of the boots she basically wore all the time now. Changed clothes. Put on the idiotic but warm pink onesie. Got into bed.

She'd no sooner climbed in than thought better of her decision, and turned to crawl to the foot of the bed to tuck in where she could watch through the windows to the sky, hoping the aurora would appear.

In the meanwhile, she grabbed a notebook and set about sorting out her life.

Lists.

Lists for work.

Lists for NASA, for those initial physicals she'd been saddled with in the interim while awaiting Tony's replacement.

Lists for the vineyard.

Lists. That was how you kept moving forward when life delivered another few gut punches.

CHAPTER EIGHT

"LIA?"

Hearing her name, complete with urgent electronic disembodiment, jerked hard on Lia's attention and her hands. She clumsily sprayed the air above the baby spinach she'd been tending in the station's greenhouse as her pulse instantly shot higher than the orbiting satellite she still planned her days around.

The radio she had been carrying like a dead weight every minute since the other doctors had left, even to the bathroom, and the shower, weighed at her hip. And until now, it hadn't so much as crackled.

She fumbled with the thing, wrestling it off her belt and looking at it for a full three seconds before remembering what she was supposed to do.

Push a button, talk, let go.

"Yes. This is Lia."

She'd no more than clicked off when her stomach did a little excited somersault and she recognized the voice.

West.

It took that long for her brain to catch up with the truth her body instantly had known.

"I need you," was all he said.

She didn't take the time to say anything else, just took advantage of the adrenaline pulsing through her body and moved faster than she would've thought herself capable.

Radio still in hand, she skittered sideways down the narrow greenhouse aisle, then ran for the corridor.

How was it even possible he was there? He left. Three days ago. He and Jordan and Zeke. Was Jordan back, too?

No. Jordan had emailed her pictures of sunny blue ocean from San Diego just this morning. Jordan was in California.

Lia hadn't stayed to watch the bus leave. Had he gotten off and just been laying low?

She didn't stop to take off the apron she wore there, just ran hard all the way to the clinic.

It wasn't far from the clinic, in the same part of the station, on the same corridor. In less than half a minute, she pushed through the swinging doors.

West stood just inside the main entry. Sort of.

He was on his feet, but both of his hands braced on the surface of the sign-in desk where a radio was located, leaning hard. Not a lazy lean. The lean of a man who didn't have the strength to stay upright without using all his limbs. Disheveled, eyes almost empty, like that second before anesthesia fully claimed consciousness.

A large, crumpled duffel bag sat on the floor a half meter away, along with the thick, regulation-issue coat he'd been wearing the last time she saw him, in the swirling snow and frosty air.

She reached him as he straightened, and immediately swayed hard to the right. He would've fallen if she hadn't grabbed him by the lapels and became a solid *something* for him to use to ground himself.

"Hey now, what's going on? West?"

One look at the blackness around his eyes and the network of red webs told her he wasn't calling because he *needed* her. He needed her. Something was wrong.

"I'm here to work," he said, then blinked hard, like his

eyes had gone out of focus and squeezing them would make the world crystal again.

"You look like it," she murmured, then began steering him backward, turning as she did until he was perched on the edge of the desk and she could safely let go. "What's going on? Have you been out in the cold all this time?"

He said it again. "I'm here to work."

Definitely not okay, and the urgent need to fix it *now* had her mentally tumbling through scenarios and noting symptoms.

"Well, it's not your shift," she said, because that was the only thing she could think to say.

"No?"

She shook her head and tried again. "Where have you been? Did you come back?"

His hands again found her hips, like it was a natural armrest, and she could tell he was struggling to come up with answers. It was a kind of fun-house mirror to their last goodbye, when words had been hard to find only because the subject was hard; these should've been easy answers.

"Dallas," he finally said, and she didn't have to do any complicated math to realize that if he'd made it to Dallas and back in three days, he'd turned around and come back almost immediately.

This was exhaustion, dangerous exhaustion, and the pauses were more likely fleeting, frequent consciousness lapses.

He needed sleep. Emergency sleep...

"Okay, well, your cabin isn't prepared, so come with me." She took his hands and stepped back, urging him to his wobbly feet. He nearly tripped over the duffel, and that was the end of the chances she was willing to take he'd make it to one of the beds. Holding his hands, while comforting in a way that could shake her insides, wouldn't help get him there. She turned in, and slung one of his arms across her shoulders so she could get him around the waist and make him lean.

"Where are we going?"

Exhaustion could mimic drunkenness, she'd once read, but she'd never seen it before today.

"Bed."

"That's good."

She got him shuffled to the closest patient bed, then turned him to sit. She immediately launched in, unfastening his suit so she could get him out of it.

If his coordination had been something under his control, she would've been stripped naked by the time she got his coveralls pooled around his waist. As it was, he kept fumbling with the zipper pull on the lighter suit she wore inside, like it was some strange contraption he'd never seen and couldn't make his fingers effectively grip.

"You'll have to do it," he muttered, clearly thinking they were up to something besides her trying to get him undressed in case of emergency. She needed his arms bare for a line and vitals.

Playing along still seemed like the easiest thing. "Okay. I'll do it later. You stand up for me? I want to get your coveralls down."

He nodded, grabbed the edge of the bed for support, and then the wall once he got upright, and she took everything down as quickly as she could, leaving him in just his boxers and the thermal shirt he'd worn beneath the coveralls.

Once more, he sat, and she stayed down there to get his boots off.

His skin always felt warm to her, but today he felt feverish. Did exhaustion cause fevers? She wasn't immediately sure. It made a kind of sense, any kind of trauma to the body could make it react with a fever, and extreme sleep deprivation was definitely a kind of trauma.

"Feet up," she said, standing and trying to swing his

legs into the bed as she did, but his heels touched down on the mattress and she felt his arms around her the next second, the world tilting.

His coordination problems aside, his mouth found hers as if guided by a laser, and the mattress at her back confirmed what he really thought was about to happen. The man was probably only technically awake, but he still had enough energy to pick her off the floor and roll.

And kiss.

Sweet mercy, the man knew how to kiss. Months since she'd felt his mouth on hers, and it was the same, saturated with that drugging euphoria he'd always been able to create with the barest brush of his lips or the glide of his tongue.

She wanted to wrap her arms around his shoulders and just let the good feelings roll over her, but there was just enough functioning gray matter left to remind her: it wasn't right. He wasn't thinking clearly. Even if he'd started this, she'd be taking advantage to let it continue. Knowing that, it still took her several long, drugging kisses before she got control enough to press his shoulders back, giving a strong enough hint for him to understand.

He leaned back just a touch, so his nose brushed hers and his quick, warm breath fanned her cheeks.

"West?"

"Hmm?" He stayed up long enough to indicate he was listening, but then leaned right back in and kissed her again, trailing little nips and suckles along her jaw to the side of her neck.

The softness of his lips, the familiar and unfamiliar crisp brush of his beard, the way his tongue slipped out to stroke her skin, it all scrambled her thoughts almost as much as sleep deprivation had scrambled his.

He didn't seem to even remember they'd broken up. Twice, basically.

She gave a little tug to the hair on the back of his head, not enough to hurt but enough to urge him back again.

"What are you doing?" she asked softly, catching his gaze when he was up again.

He smiled, eyes half-closed, a dreamlike happiness flowing off him. "Snogging you senseless."

Had he ever looked at her that way? Unguarded and open and…it looked like love. God, she really didn't know how to tell what love looked like. He'd told her he didn't love her. He'd made it very clear.

Maybe they were both confused. Maybe he was mentally in those few days before Charlie had died…and he hadn't come to whatever realization had prompted him leaving.

Jerking him out of somewhere so happy felt awful, but she had to stop this.

She nodded to his simple, adorable answer, and when he leaned in to kiss her again, she turned her head.

Undeterred, he continued nuzzling and nibbling, and her foggy brain came to another realization. He wasn't trying to get her naked. This was cuddling. Kissing just to kiss? Not how they usually operated.

But she wished it had been. It was as sexy as it was sweet.

And she had to stop it. "Why?"

"Why am I kissing you?"

"Mmm-hmm…"

He pulled back again, still happy. Amused, even. "You suddenly don't like kissing me?"

God, she didn't want to do this. And she couldn't do it with the warm, solid weight of him pressing her into the bed, when every instinct said it was right. She got some traction in the mattress and slid up just a little, his gaze still tracking her, befuddled.

She couldn't just blurt out, *Remember how you don't*

love me and ran two hemispheres to get away? It might be true, but it would be like kicking a puppy at this point.

"Where are we?" she asked instead.

Still confused, he looked up and at the room briefly before focusing on her again. "You don't want to kiss at work?"

Not about what she wanted. By the saints, she wanted to stay right there with him, kissing, cuddling, everything...

She tried again. "Where are we?"

"Medical ward?"

Good. This might work. Without unnecessary cruelty. "Right. Where is that?"

He caught on that she was leading him somewhere, and his answers became slower and, for the moment, more confused. "Fletcher?"

"That's right." She puffed, watching him slowly starting to catch up. "Where is Fletcher?"

"Antarctica."

It was getting through. He leaned up just a little bit, clearly picking up that he was missing something, but not sure what yet.

"Why are we in Antarctica?" she asked finally.

She could see the second it clicked. His brow softened, then went slack. A look of undisguised grief bloomed in his eyes for an earth-stopping second, then he was moving, rolling off her.

"Lia... I'm sorry. I don't... I don't know..."

She slid off the bed and, once on her feet, turned to urge him back against the bed; doing things had a way of letting her feel in control. Or at least let her cover her lack of it. "It's okay. Why did you come back?"

"I had to," he said softly, his eyelids drooping.

"Why?"

Eyes closed, and mouth that had been working so beautiful started getting sluggish. "Didn'…have anywhere else…to go."

He'd be asleep in a moment. If she wanted answers, she needed to get them now. Even if it just sounded like he'd slammed her with the truth she knew he didn't realize he was saying. Like a drunken confession, but with a fever.

He wouldn't have been allowed to just come back on his own. He'd have to have arranged it, gotten permission. People didn't just get to visit Antarctic research stations without a job waiting for them or maybe special permission. There wasn't any other way to get there than through the actual official transport. He'd gotten permission, and came straight back.

"Are you taking over Tony's study?"

He opened his eyes, and nodded. "Yes. That's why I came back."

The official line. He probably didn't even realize he'd said something else a moment ago. Both reasons might be facts, but the first? That was *truth*. And that made her heart ache, too.

"Did you sleep at all while you were gone?"

"Couple hours in Dallas."

"Hotel?"

"Airport."

So, no rest really.

"Did you sleep on the plane at all?"

"Don' remember," he mumbled. She could almost see reality shrinking in his eyes.

"Boat? West?"

He shrugged, eyes closed again.

Basically, no sleep for three days on top of a few days with a couple of hours here and there, and thousands of miles of extensive, arduous travel. Amazing he'd made it at all.

Why would he do that? They would've let him recover

a couple of days in Dallas before getting on another plane. There was time, at least a couple of weeks left before travel would become all but impossible.

She couldn't keep him awake any longer. "Let me get that shirt off you, and then you can sleep. I'm going to get your vitals, okay?"

He leaned up and she helped him out of the long-sleeved shirt, and when he laid back again, he said nothing else, breathing slow, regular and deep.

He hadn't answered, but he also hadn't said no. She'd be failing to take proper care of a patient if she didn't check him out.

She grabbed the nurse on a stick and went to work.

Temperature, elevated.

Pulse oxygen levels, great.

Blood pressure, also elevated.

Through it all, he didn't so much as flinch, sleeping hard enough to add to her concern.

Fever could be an illness, sign of either a bacterial or viral infection. Or it could be unrelated, and all about his lack of sleep.

A blood panel would make her feel better about letting him sleep it off...

Five minutes later, she'd drawn several vials of blood, which he'd also slept through, and she went to run it for results, one thought circling her brain: *he came back*.

If he hadn't been so clear about not loving her, she'd have taken it for a chance to not be *done*. But it was far more likely that she was the excuse that allowed him to come back, when the truth was more about his rootless existence. She may not want to live in Portugal full-time due to the expectations placed on her there, but she always could go there when she needed to. She was always welcome, even if that was also where she'd be reminded she was a disappointment. She had a fail-safe, break-in-case-of-emergency home to return to. It didn't seem like he did.

More worrying still, for a man who lived in the future and delighted in his future plans, him not having future plans to go to said something else was very wrong.

How had Charlie died?

CHAPTER NINE

BATHROOM.

The driving need for a bathroom dragged West from sleep.

Before opening his eyes, he swiveled and rolled, lifting the blankets as he went, but half turned, felt a tug at his arm and a little pinch of pain.

He froze, opened his sluggish eyes, and a hospital room came into focus.

Patient room. Fletcher.

He laid back again, surveying his body as he did.

IV in left arm, lightly stinging.

Hospital gown.

Need for a bathroom…

He lifted the blanket and peered beneath. A catheter line laid across his thigh.

Damn it.

He didn't need a bathroom. It just *felt* like he needed a bathroom.

Lia.

Her face swam up in his mind, pillows behind her head, cheeks pink. Lips pink…

Hell. He'd kissed her. In this bed. More than kissed, but less than he'd wanted to do. Still wanted to do, but was now in control enough to remember that he had no right to touch her. Not like that. Not anymore. Not after what he'd done.

How had he forgotten what they were now?

Always.

He groaned and flopped his head back against the pillow as the word came swimming back to him.

He'd been out of his mind, and plowed under by that one word rolling through his brain on repeat over thousands of miles. *Sempre.* Always.

In the next instant, he heard running and Lia appeared in the doorway, eyes wide, assessing.

"Catheter? Really?" he asked, then mentally kicked himself. Should've said something else. All the time gone, he'd only thought about that one word. *Sempre. Always.*

He'd abandoned her again, lied ugly, and she'd said *always* to him.

"You've been asleep…unwakeable—" she stopped to check her watch "—for almost twenty-one hours."

"Twenty-one hours?" he repeated, the words not seeming possible. "Since I got back? Twenty-one hours?"

She nodded, and he looked a little closer as she neared the bed. There was a hint of darkness under her eyes, made more noticeable by how peely-wally she looked. Tired. Exhausted. But *relieved.*

She moved around his bed to check his IV, the drip rate, the amount of saline left on the pole. "You had a fever, and you fell asleep while I was checking your vitals."

"And?"

"Elevated blood pressure. I did a blood panel, which you also slept through, and ran it. Dehydration, elevated white count, and I was worried about dehydration, so I ran a line. A few hours later, when you still refused to wake up, I decided to set the Foley."

He didn't need to do anything but look into her eyes to see how worried she'd been. Still was. And he wasn't sure how to explain it to her. How he even explained it to himself.

Leaving had felt like dying. Like a mistake. Like another abandonment. If he left her here and something happened to her—he'd heard stories about how dangerous things could get in the winter. There were self-contained, survival pods dubbed lifeboats all over the station for a reason.

If something happened to her and he wasn't there...that would be the end of him. No matter where he was, that would be the end. Words he couldn't just blurt out to her.

Stay on point. The catheter. Just thinking the one word, he felt it again, and couldn't help wincing. "It's my first. I have new sympathy for patients who've complained about them in the past."

She grinned a touch, nodding. "I know."

"What else?"

"I did another panel a couple of hours ago. White cells decreased. I think you're on the mend."

His body bounced back faster than his mind.

"Let's check vitals again," she said. She wheeled the mobile tool caddy to his bedside, and he let her get on with it. "If your pressure looks good, and you feel like it, I'll bring a kit for you to deflate the Foley's balloon and remove it. I just didn't want to leave it when you were so far gone and I was pumping you full of fluids."

"Thanks," he said as she took the thermometer back and made a note of all the readings.

It was a matter of dignity, letting him handle it. She certainly had done a myriad of far more pleasurable things with his penis, but this was different.

And that intimacy had been before, when they were together, and they weren't now. Something he'd had to admit had to change. A faulty plan, at least once he'd seen her again. She was harder to walk away from in the flesh... with those big pretty eyes full of dashed hopes.

"I'll get the kit," she said, taking the mobile vitals trolley with her to the door. "But wait for me to get back before you get up."

"I was pretty bad, eh?"

"I'm not sure how we got you into the bed." She stopped at the door to look at him again, not mentioning his obvious mental break when he'd been a horny zombie at his return. "Are you feeling okay?"

Not really.

"I'm fine," he lied. Physically, he felt fine, but the rest? Conflicted about the deal he'd made with himself that allowed him to return, to even try to put things back together with her. "Just never slept so long before. Kind of hungover. And trying to think of what I can even say to you."

She nodded, the worry in her eyes spiking for a moment, then settling again into that same tired concern. She'd heard him, and didn't want to acknowledge the spiky topic. She focused on his health. "Headache?"

"No. Just sluggish, or something. And both amazed and dismayed to have needed such tending."

"You don't need to say anything. You'd have looked after me, too."

Either purposefully taking his words to be about gratitude rather than confession, or unaware it could be anything else.

"I abandoned you, Lia."

The word made her breath hitch, then her mouth actually turned down at the corners. The soft plushness he couldn't get enough of compressed with the ghost of worry and exhaustion. And again, she dodged it. "I'll get the kit and go to the galley to bring back lunch."

Before he said another word, she buzzed off to tick off her tasks, leaving what he needed to rid himself of the Foley, and disappearing.

He set to work with the syringe at the port to draw the saline out of it, and then took a deep breath, and pulled.

It came out, and with it, a relieved breath.

Always stayed there, in his mouth, ready to come out every time he spoke, but that seemed like something he should work up to, as well. He couldn't expect her to just take him back because he'd returned. All sins required penance.

The rest of the words—words he didn't understand or remember—seemed to be as hope-filled to him. But the foreign sounds hadn't stayed with him long enough to be translated. He'd drained the battery on his phone trying to string together what he remembered of the sounds to create faux Portuguese words for a translation app to work with, and got nothing. Tried to reverse engineer with guesses in English, but none of that had looked right, either.

Not the direct, traditional words of a love confession. He knew how to say *I love you* in Portuguese: *amo-te*.

But he'd heard the emotion in her voice, seen it in her eyes. Nothing else fit with whispered goodbyes and teary cheek-kisses.

He wanted the IV gone, to be as right as he could be, before she got back, and he didn't need it now. On the opposite wall to his bed sat a cabinet where he found those supplies, then returned to the bed.

When he'd left London, it had hurt both of them, but it had felt surgical. Curative. Better for her in the long run.

This time, he'd hated himself before he'd even set foot on the transport bus. Known too well what he was putting her through—the torment of yet another abandonment, because that's what it was. That's what it had been both times. And he knew more about that particular pain than he'd wish for anyone.

But he'd still done it.

She came back with a tray of food and a tall glass of lemonade, placed both on a rolling bedside table and scooted to him. "Eat and then walk?"

He nodded, leaning back, unable to keep himself from looking at her—watching her look at his arm, the supplies where he'd removed the line and the cotton ball he'd already taped it down with.

"Or did you already get up?"

One more pointed look at the cabinet and back.

"Two steps is barely walking," he said, still holding her gaze and the unspoken questions he saw there.

"Wobbly?"

"Not too bad. I'm not a falls risk."

"No bed alarm needed?" She half smiled, trying to joke, set things on a more even keel with them, but he couldn't go along with it. Not now.

"Too many other kinds of alarms."

His words made her freeze, just a few seconds, and then she resumed gathering up the remains of the medical supplies he'd used to remove the uncomfortable implements, and looked at him. "Did you return to make me leave, or to fill Tony's position? Why are you back, West?"

"Always," he answered, paying no attention to the food she'd placed before him. Finding out what she'd said was more important than hunger. "That's the only word you said outside the bus that I understood. *Sempre.* Always."

Her breathing picked up. She looked away, removing the trash, then maintaining the distance from him, like she needed some air between them to take whatever he was going to say. Or to give her the courage to answer. "They were the only words that came."

"What were they?"

She licked her lips, obviously wary of answering. Then slowly, with pauses between each word, lacking her customary rapid manner of speaking her native tongue, said, *"Eu...sempre...terei...saudades...de ti."*

Despite the slowness, there was no nervous quality to the admission, just a heavy-eyed sense of vulnerability that said she knew she was exposing a lot. That he had asked a lot of her repeating it.

"Terry...sawdadesh..." He repeated the sounds back, trying on the feel of them and no doubt bungling them up. Making her answer his as-yet-unasked question.

"There is no direct translation. The closest is...'I'll miss you.'"

"Always?"

She flushed then, but nodded. "That word has a direct translation."

"Where does the other fall short?"

"Saudades." She said the word again. "It's like home-sickness. In the soul. Usually for a place."

She waited to see if that explanation was enough.

It wasn't. If there was more, he needed to hear it. He waited.

"Terei saudades." She said the word again, shaking her head, voice falling back to her usual softness. "I have... missing feelings...that...can never be healed...by anything else. And I am broken by it."

Her voice rasped over the end, and when she leaned off the wall to make her exit, he saw tears in her eyes again.

His own eyes burned, his chest on fire.

"Lia..."

She stopped in the doorway, her gaze falling to the floor, not to him again. Waiting...

"I'm not worthy of those feelings."

"You don't get to decide that," she cut in, shaking her head, a little sniff preceding her swiping her cheeks. "You practically killed yourself getting back here when there was time for you to rest. Did they refuse to let you have a day of rest before getting onto another plane?"

"No. But you were the only doctor here. You saw how many people have gotten hurt this week while they've been shuttering parts of the station for the first time."

She didn't exactly roll her eyes at him, but the exaggerated slow blink had the same damned effect, and she folded her arms. Didn't believe him. "Are we done?"

Done with this conversation, or *done*?

He didn't ask, just felt the wave of nausea as his empty stomach churned, and he lifted one hand on instinct to touch his throat, searching and not finding the necklace and her ring.

In the silence, she came back to the bedside, hand dipping into one pocket. When she pulled it free, the chain and ring dangled from her fingers.

"Didn't want you choking yourself in your sleep, the way you usually move around. But then you didn't move at all."

"Twenty-one hours?" he repeated, the number still shocking, but took the offered ring.

"Twenty-one hours," she confirmed, then walked away again. "Welcome back, Dr. MacIntyre. Eat. You need to get your strength back."

Always, she'd said, and he'd still bungled it up.

At no other time in his life had anyone cared…had anyone loved him enough to track him down once he'd gone. Even his brother. But she'd gone halfway around the world for him, and even if she was rightfully wary of him now, she still loved him.

He had to say something now. It was one of those times he couldn't play it cool and wait, plan what to say.

"I'm not worthy of your feelings," he repeated, and she stopped again in the doorway, her back to him, "but I want them. You. And I'm selfish enough to admit it."

"Why?" she asked, not turning back.

"Charlie overdosed. I wasn't there," he said softly. It was easier to talk to her back. He could say words he'd never had the heart to utter aloud before, without having to look in her eyes and see her opinion of him sink. Just enough to try to explain.

"In the States?" she asked, half turning back toward him, her face a perfect combination of horror and compassion.

"I lied to you about where he was. I couldn't get him clean, and I was ashamed of my addict little brother. So. Not the States. Near Glasgow."

If she took him back, he'd probably have to tell her the whole story someday. Before they got to the rings and vows again. Somehow. But giving details meant picturing it, and he did everything he could not to picture it.

"Were you angry with me for not being there? I would've come back. I would've gone with you…"

"I know you would've. It's not that. Not your fault," he said, his accent thicker when he spoke while searching for the words than when he was fully in control of himself. "I'm still tryin' to work out how to deal with it. So, just to be fair to you, I'm goin' to say that I don' know if I can be what you need. I know I lied to you, I failed you, and that you probably shouldn' trust me. I'm far too good at breaking things."

CHAPTER TEN

HE WANTED HER BACK.

Before West had revealed how he felt and *didn't* feel about her, Lia had harbored quiet fantasies of getting back together. But since then, even knowing that she'd only days ago questioned why he hadn't wanted to keep seeing her and see if love developed, standing on the other side of it felt different. Scary.

Saying *yes* would mean entering an unequal relationship, where she loved him, but he didn't, and may never love her back. How long was she supposed to even give that kind of a trial?

She didn't want to be that stupid again, and had already proven she couldn't even correctly identify love. She confused it with general happiness, and probably lust. Would she ever be able to believe him if he said the words to her again?

"I don't want to sound cruel, and I don't want to have a fight in the clinic, but I won't lead you on, either. I don't know why you want me back when you've been very clear that you never loved me. I didn't realize it before, I didn't think anyone would propose without love, so I believed it. But the truth is I don't have any idea what that feels like."

"What *what* feels like?"

"Being loved. You say you want me, and I believe you do because want doesn't require more than physical connection—something we're very good at." Or had been before. They'd been too wounded and cagey since she'd returned to do more than feel things, and then stuff them away. "But you *don't* love me, so I don't know. I need to think about it, about whether we can have something healthy and happy." She licked her lips and shook her head. "I'm glad you're here. I don't really believe that you came back for me, but I am glad you're here."

"When I said—"

"No," she cut him off. "I don't want to talk about this more right now. You need to eat and get a walk in before I'm willing to discharge you." She opened her mouth to say more, but a loud, frantic cry for help from the lobby took precedence, and sent her sluggish heart back into instant overdrive.

Without another word, she turned and ran toward the voice.

"What happened?" West heard Lia say through the opened door.

"He's not breathing. I found him like this…" a man said.

West took two big bites of the noodles she'd brought him, then shoved the table aside and got up to fetch a second gown from the cabinet to use as a robe and conceal his backside. He hadn't gotten around to asking where his clothes were, and he was going to go help, with or without them.

"Air was really thin in there," the man said as West made it out, breathing labored, and had obviously carried the patient in. He stood to the side, hands gripped together, worriedly watching.

"Where was it?" West asked. They'd gotten the man on the table and Lia was climbing up to straddle him, fingers linked to begin chest compressions.

"Mechanical room."

Another injury from Mechanical?

"Thin air," she puffed between compressions, but he heard her flinging open drawers to get a mouth guard out to breathe for him when she stopped.

He took and delivered two quick breaths before she resumed. "I know."

Suffocation could do that, if the room was pressure sealed, but why would Mechanical be pressure sealed?

"Oxygen?" he prompted, and she nodded, but didn't speak again, focused on applying the proper amount of pressure, and keeping count. Chest compressions were a workout and carried on for a long time. It was common to need to switch out with someone fresh, so the cadence wouldn't be affected. Exhaustion could set in quickly when someone was fully rested, let alone whatever state Lia was in.

He kept an eye on her, and breathed for the man when he was supposed to, mentally ticking through what else it could be. Carbon monoxide was a silent killer, odorless, and breathing didn't feel affected up until it was too late. So it was unlikely to be noticed as thin air, but did sound like something that could actually happen in Mechanical with the machines and exhaust.

Regardless, the treatment was the same. Pure oxygen would help, if anything was going to.

He dug out a laryngoscope, bag valve ventilator, and connected it straight into the oxygen in seconds, readying himself to dive in and intubate the man the next time she stopped.

"He's still warm," she said, which was something at least. And as soon as she counted her last compression, she helped tilt his head back to lengthen the throat, and West slid in the blade and tubing, then began pumping straight oxygen into the man's lungs.

Three puffs, an extra to help, and she resumed.

After the fourth set of full oxygen breaths, the mechanical aeration of the man's blood worked. His head jerked once, and she stopped to feel the pulse in his throat, her hands shaking, and following up, he could see her arms shaking, too. Not nerves, but weakness that came from overexertion, because if anyone was going to have one of those TV doctor moments of having to be dragged away from a patient who was too far gone, it would be Lia. She'd keep going until he made her stop. Or until they got lucky.

She didn't climb down yet, instead grabbing the man's wrists to pin beneath her knees, in case he should wake and do what most people did when they woke up intubated—try to pull it out. He needed the oxygen. If this was carbon monoxide poisoning, he'd need hours of pure, undiluted oxygen.

They waited and watched for a full minute, but when he didn't fully rouse, she climbed down and they got his manual pump respirator switched to the machine and began attaching leads to monitor his heart.

"Thinking someone needs to get a detector down there." She breathed hard. "And we need to get him stable and out of here. His sternum cracked, and he'll need a lot of care for a while."

"If he wakes," West said softly. They both knew his chances weren't great.

"While the weather allows travel, we need to relocate him. Is there anywhere in South America with a hyperbaric chamber? Or maybe a navy boat?"

"I don't know." He didn't, but he would find out. "I've read that they help filter the blood, but there's no evidence that it helps."

"There's no evidence that it doesn't," she grumbled, breathing starting to even out, but she still shook as if by an internal earthquake.

The man they'd been ignoring made himself known

again. "Does it always make you die? If you've got carbon monoxide poisoning?"

West glanced sideways at Lia, and despite still being in a hospital gown, he said to the man, "You went in after him?"

A nod was his answer, and he shared a look with Lia to let her know he was handling it.

"Let's check you out. You might benefit from some oxygen, too."

Still focused on their main patient, she didn't interfere, but did call after him, "Get blood."

"Get my clothes when you're done," he called back, ushering the man into an exam room. "How are you feeling? Anything off? And what's your name? I can't pull up your file—I don't have a device—but I can check this right now."

"Mario Correa," he answered first. "I haven't been feeling right since the day I moved into Pod A."

"Not about Mechanical?" West asked, and when the man shrugged, he continued. "Symptoms?"

"I don't know. Tired and off," Mario said, then looked at West seriously. "Doctor, are you sure you're well enough for this? Maybe the lady doctor should see me."

"I'm okay," West assured him. "I've been discharged, just haven't gotten changed yet. So, after sleeping in Pod A you felt poorly?"

"It was before bed," he said. "I worked in the shop all day that day. Actually, it was the day after we'd shut down Pod B, where I had been, and some other parts of the station. I went to Mechanical to make a part for the ventilation system so we could change it."

"Repair?"

"Not broken, but the engineers came up with some way to save energy, and that meant closing down different parts

than they'd originally planned. So we're reworking ventilation and electrical, those kinds of things."

Right. None of that meant much to him.

"We'll get some blood. That'll tell us if you've got a
carbon monoxide concentration. But I'm going to get you
on oxygen now, just in case."

"How does that help?"

"Pushes the carbon monoxide out of the blood. It takes a
few hours to clean it out, but we can do that. You just have
to wear a mask and breathe only the oxygen that comes
through it," he explained, getting the man set up and turning the oxygen flow on. "It smells kind of weird, but it'll
help. If you can, lie down on the table and nap after I get
your blood. If it's clear, I'll let you go. If it's not, you stay
until it is."

"I need to call my boss…"

"I'll get it," West said, getting that information from the
man to make the call. It sounded to him like something
weird was going on with ventilation, but it was a new station and this was the first time being overwintered. It was
bound to have kinks that needed working out as things
were used and bugs discovered.

He'd find Lia after. Get some clothes. Finish their conversation before sending her to bed. He'd slept twenty-
one hours; he could stay awake for another eight so she
could sleep.

It was fine. They had time. They weren't *done*. Even
if he'd made this exponentially harder with his lie about
having never loved her. A lie he still couldn't believe she'd
bought, no more than he could believe her assertion that
she'd never been loved, that she didn't know what it felt
like.

Jordan loved her. Her friends. Certainly her family and
the people in her village. Unless that was the big mess she'd
wanted to keep him away from.

* * *

It was funny the things that occurred to Lia in the middle of an emergency. How it was possible to save a life with CPR eleven percent of the time if you performed the right steps, the right way, in the right amount of time after the last natural respiration.

Maybe in eleven percent of alternate universes, he said those words to her and it saved their relationship. And maybe the reason she'd been gritting her teeth all afternoon was how badly she wanted to take him back, and how bad an idea she knew that to be. But it would feel good in the moment.

All is forgiven.

Pretend nothing happened.

Pretend she didn't remember the *other* words he'd said.

What she couldn't work out was why he'd said them. And why hadn't *she*?

She could've lied, or just told him she didn't want to translate the words she'd said outside the bus, when she hadn't expected to ever have to own up to them. And couldn't bring herself to lie about them. Which could be something she did need to learn.

Instead, she'd spent hours trying to convince herself that this new pragmatism was a sign of growth. That she was just uncovering the real Lia.

She'd kept busy after resuscitation, arranging transport to get her resus patient back to civilization and the care he'd need. And where his family could go to him, where they wouldn't have to worry if he was all right.

West had gotten changed and dumped his belongings off at his new cabin in Pod A, no longer next door for her to worry about, then returned after dinner.

"I'm going to take the night shift so you can get some sleep," he said from the door to the office. She'd expected to have the rest of the evening to herself, to gather her wits, but there he was.

She fisted her hands in her lap, trying to hide her white-knuckling it through the conversation, a twisting grip on her jacket better than the grip she had on her willpower. Shoving him out of the office and yelling at him would probably be a bad thing, especially as he was now there to work. And she didn't even know if Kasey was running the transport bus now to escape.

"You don't have to. I'll set alarms, keep a radio with me and go check on him every hour…"

"Why?"

"It's my job. I don't want you thinking you have to take care of me. Or that it will change things. We both probably need to stay in our lanes for a few days."

He made some sound of understanding, then moseyed in to lean against her desk. "So, by our lanes, you mean no hugging, no relationship talk, no random love declarations or trying to give you the ring back?"

"For instance," she said, but felt herself bristling when he said "love declarations." Her nails digging into her palms made her pull them from her lap and reach for an ink pen on her desk instead. Something to fidget with that wouldn't hurt.

He played it too cool, but when she looked up at him, she saw worry in his brow. Another thing she couldn't count on reading correctly. Instinct wanted to believe that you couldn't worry about someone you didn't love, but that wasn't true. She was worried about her resus patient, someone she'd just met while unconscious.

"For instance?"

"It would be counterproductive to comment further, and definitely strays outside of what my lane should be right now when I'm trying to picture what this is going to be like, working together in close quarters for eight months," she grumbled, giving voice to what was in her head, because why not? "Besides, it would be a lie, wouldn't it?"

"What would be a lie?"

"Love declarations," she repeated, then looked up at him, not ready to back down on that one. "It feels manipulative when you say things like that, given what I know. You never loved me. So, if you didn't love me before, when I was actively trying to be what you wanted, you certainly don't love me now."

"I did love you," he argued, then, "You were trying to be what I wanted?"

"I always try to be what I think people I love want me to be. Everyone does it. Some better than others." Her energy flagged, because it had been an exhausting couple of days, and that was before the morning CPR. "And you didn't. You told me you didn't. You practically said it again when you told me to not cry because you dislike me having red eyes."

"That's not why I said that." He looked kind of bewildered, and that just made her want to cry again. "I lied. I lied about Charlie, I lied about loving you. And you know what? There's more. I don't... There's..."

He stopped and pinched the bridge of his nose, eyes closing. "It seemed like the kindest thing to do at the time. I did love you. I *do* love you, as well as I'm able."

"Even if I wanted to believe that, I know it's not true. How can you really love me when you don't even know me?"

"Of course I know you."

"You don't know me. *I* don't even know me." She threw her hands up, her voice rising with them, but through her evident exhaustion, she remembered where they were and lowered her voice again. "We went over this. It's just rehashing at this point. If you loved anything, it was on the surface, or what you thought we would become sometime in the future. When plans worked out. Living the dream. But I can't do that anymore. I'm making changes, which no one seems to notice, anyway, so why are we even having this discussion?"

"By changes, you mean being grumpy?"

"Growing my hair out. Wearing pink things. Not forcing myself to project optimism that I don't feel, though I guess that's the same as grumpy." She stood up to mostly close the door, leaving it open enough to hear if anyone called for help.

"Of course I noticed the changes, but what does a haircut or pink pajamas have to do with who you are as a person?"

"We all have reasons for the things we do. Even if they're stupid reasons, we all have reasons. My father is on the run because he doesn't want to deal with the vineyard anymore, or the mess. And maybe so he doesn't have to see me succeed with it, because I will. Reasons are important for the things we do."

"There's a deeper reason behind growing your hair out than you simply want to change your hair?"

"Yes," she said, then went to check the radios on their charging stations, to see if they were getting a full charge. "And the reason I'm calling this conversation to a close right now is that I'm tired. And disillusioned. And wishing I had a superpower right now."

He chuckled. "What superpower would that be?"

She nodded toward the door. "Heal him."

"Ah, see, that's why you're a better doctor than I am," he said, and when she turned to look at him, he reached out to take her hand. "Do you want to know what superpower I want to have?"

"No," she said instantly, the way he looked into her eyes and stroked her hand giving her a silly little turn in the conversation gravity. "What?"

"Time-travel," he said softly. "But I can't fix the past. All I can try to do is do better. We have eight months to work this out, don't we? I'm not a patient man, so don't expect me to just give up and wait, but I can do something for you tonight, and take the night shift, keep an eye on our patient so you can get eight hours. I think after twenty-one hours of straight sleep I can manage that."

She opened her mouth to argue, but suddenly couldn't think of why. Instead, she nodded her agreement, and when he tugged her over to wrap his arms around her, she leaned in. But she couldn't bring herself to put her arms around him in return. Her hands and cheek rested against his chest, and he propped his bearded chin atop her pink knitted hat, and there they stood, swaying together for far too long.

Up close, she could see the shape of her ring under the thermal shirt he wore, and felt that pit open back up in her stomach.

Hugging was definitely to be avoided. And she'd tell him that, too. Tomorrow.

CHAPTER ELEVEN

WEST WAITED UNTIL THEN, when it was likely that Lia would wake up on her own and be ticked at him, before he elbow-knocked on her door.

From the cacophony that preceded her opening the door, he could only assume that the new layout of the cabin was throwing her.

"G'mornin'…" He gave his best smile, then stretched out the hand holding her gadgets. "Brought these back."

"Brought back?" she repeated, then picked them up as if they were foreign gizmos she'd never seen before. "Did I leave them out?"

He shook his head, then held out the mug of tea he'd brought in offering. "I came in and stole them last night so you could get a little extra sleep. Have tea, and get woken up a little. I've had a whole night of thinking, and you know I'm an impatient man."

She took both offerings, pausing to toss the phone and radio behind her onto the bed, but kept the steaming mug in her hands. "You came and took them?"

"Aye," he said, then nodded. "And I'm on duty still. It's only ten, so I need to make this quick. May I come in?"

Last evening, he'd seen her run the emotional gamut from sad, to incredulous, to seriously annoyed, to far too quiet. It was the last one that had stayed with him. The one that had informed this morning's decision.

"Why?" she asked, still not awake. Still adorably squinty-faced and now missing a hat, he could see how much her hair had grown out. Something he needed to ask her about. Those reasons she'd so passionately referenced.

"Because I have to say something…"

Last night, he hadn't been able to properly appreciate how much roomier these quarters were, or the view. The room might end up colder than the ones at the end of the pods, as one wall had an immense, outwardly bending bubble of a window. Could've been on a submarine, or one of those retro midcentury designs for what they expected the future to look like: all modern lines and bubble windows. Would be hard to cover in the summer. Which might account for some of Tony's insomnia. But that wasn't why he was here.

He closed the door behind her and waited for her to take a perch on the corner of the bed with her cup, then just launched into it. He was rubbish at talking about bad things, and doing it like ripping off a bandage seemed the cleanest way. Put it on the table, then go back to work.

Confessing during your morning break, it was also kind of safer. No long drawn-out discussions could happen in such a short time period.

"I thought about this all night, and as far as I could come up with, I have only two options on how to handle this," he said. "I can repeat myself until you punch me in the junk, which is neither productive nor fun. For me. Might be fun for you, depending on how angry you are."

"Pretty angry."

He nodded. "Or I can explain why I do…stupid things."

That didn't get a verbal response. She just looked instantly worried, and as alert as someone who'd been up for hours, and smartly stretched across the bed to put her tea down on the bedside table.

When she resumed a normal seated position before him,

he instantly regretted not having tried to script it out, be eloquent.

"The reason I always look forward is because my rear view is... Pompeii, Sumatra and San Francisco, you know?"

"Volcanos?"

"Catastrophes. Earth-moving catastrophes," he explained, already off to a banging start. "Only most of the catastrophes I see when I look back have been my own doin'. So, I don't like to look back. I don't like to talk about it, any of it. Or think about it. Or answer questions. Because of that, I've given you the impression I don't want to know you. I still want to believe that none of that in the past matters, only what people can build together, but that hasn't worked out so well."

She shook her head, still saying nothing, and still worried, though he could see a spark of hope growing in her eyes.

"I shut down subjects I think might lead back to those things I don't want to talk about. I know it's a coping mechanism, but it's helped me get over a lot of bad since I was a boy—focusing on the next good thing to replace the current *bad* thing."

He paused to make sure she was still with him, but before she could say anything, he held up one finger to let her know there was more coming.

"When your city is buried under tons of ash, all you can do—the easiest thing, the *cleanest* thing you can do—is move on and start over." God, he hoped she didn't start asking for details on those bad things.

"How many times?" she asked, taking advantage of the pause he had to make to take a breath and get ready to say the big thing, the thing he prayed she'd hear and believe.

It only took him a couple seconds' consideration to

know he couldn't possibly put a number to it. "I don't know the answer to that. But that's not the point, love."

She frowned, but nodded in a way that said she was going to let him continue for now, but she wasn't done with the number-of-moves thing.

He stepped closer, then squatted down so he was on eye level with her sitting on the corner of her bed. "I never look back at what's been buried. When I said I never loved you, I thought you needed to hear that so that you could move on, too. But it was a lie. And I really need you to hear this…"

She nodded slowly, and waited, but the completely undisguised fear he saw in her eyes almost made him turn back. Illuminated another instance where he understood how much he'd hurt her.

"Besides the death of my brother," he said, his throat thickening, and he could feel the water coming to his eyes, "*You* are the only disaster I've ever wanted to dig out from and rebuild." He licked his lips, nodding, as much to himself as for her to see. "I do want that."

"West…" She said his name, but he could see it wasn't going to be followed up with other words. It was shock, and joy, and sorrow rolled into one syllable, and a year's worth of feeling in her eyes.

"I know I referred to you as a disaster, and maybe that's not the best romantic thing to say, but it was over in my mind, and there was no going back. So, not artful, but—"

She shot forward, arms shooting out to wrap around his shoulders. He would've fallen, but even in these more spacious quarters, he still only had a few inches behind him of space before the wall caught them both, then it was only a matter of straightening his legs to slide his back up the door, and pull them both to their feet. It was either that, or lie down with her in the floor, and if he did that, more would follow. And no one would be minding the clinic.

"You don't have to say anything. I know it's…kind of a lot to put on you first thing when you wake, but if you decide you want to give it another go—today, two months from now or the day we leave to go back to the world—I will say yes and count myself lucky."

She nodded, and as much as he didn't want to move from where they stood, arms locked around one another, he said, "No one's mindin' the store. I should get back out there."

Although her arms loosened, she didn't let go, actually cupping his shoulders to hold on to him. "Wait. I need to know…about the moves."

"That matters?"

"Yes. I don't understand—how can you not know how many times you've made big moves?"

The number wasn't important, but the reason it was so high… Yeah, she was right about the reasons. "I'll think about it, see if I can make a list. But give me a time frame. Does that just mean as an adult? Or as a child, too?"

"Is it more than five times?"

He nodded. "Let me work on that number, right? You get ready for work, have your lunch, then you can come on duty. I'll hold the fort until. Maybe later I'll have a figure for you."

He wouldn't have a figure later, but he would make generalizations which might give her an even bigger shock. Later. He'd worry about it later.

A hug wasn't a promise. He couldn't just take the ring off the chain at his neck and slide it back onto her finger, but it was something.

Lia had said her goodbye to West outside of Kasey's bus less than a week ago, but it could've been months. Or even a different lifetime, and different people.

She hadn't even gone on duty today until around noon,

and now, at the end of the day and having seen him exactly once in the hours in between, it could've been a week. Like a child counting down to Christmas, she'd counted half-hour increments until she'd be off official duty, and could talk to him alone again. Because she'd had some thoughts, once her brain kicked back in. And they were good thoughts. They might not sound like some kind of Highland poetry as his words had done, but no one could compete with that.

So, at half past six, she'd called for him over the radio, doing her utmost to sound terribly official, asking him to come speak with her. So probably everyone now knew it was anything but official, but when *everyone* was fifty-six other people, it didn't much matter.

A knock came within minutes to her private cabin door and she peeked out quickly, noticed him there looking curious and like he'd fallen for the officiality. She also took note there was no one in the clinic to see them, grabbed his sleeve and pulled him inside.

She had taken off her insulated suit, the thin one she even tended to wear inside, and set up the heater he'd brought her to get the room warm. Because it was time for dinner, and she wanted to be alone with him, she'd laid out a little picnic on the bed, with grub from the galley. Stuff that wouldn't wreck her bedclothes if a dish tilted. Mostly hearty sandwiches and sides light on sauces.

He took all this in silently, then gave a cautious smile before asking, "So, are we picking up right where we left off? Before it all went badly wrong?"

"Not exactly," she said, then felt the need to add, "Because we are changing things, right?"

"We are." He punctuated his quiet words with a single nod, but then followed up. "Is it going to throw a wrench in the works if I steal a kiss before we get started changing things? You wouldn't…mind terribly, would you?"

And when he said it that way, with a quirk to his mouth and his head tilted so his blue eyes were full of meaningful sidelong flirting, she couldn't say no.

She leaned in to meet him halfway, intending a quick kiss of greeting, but he steered her backward until her back was against the door, and cupped both of her cheeks to press the sweetest, slowest kiss to her lips.

West's kisses always made statements. Usually, that statement was *I want you. Right now.* Sometimes the statement was *I want you and I'm cranky that I have to wait because of Reasons.*

But at that moment, the statement could not have more clearly been anything but *I missed you.*

Tenho saudades…tambem.

There may have been shades of *I love you* in that kiss. She couldn't be sure if it was there, or if she just really wanted it to be there.

Like with all their kisses when alone, soon even a sweet, lingering, loving kiss heated up. Deepened. Got them both a little stupid.

Just when she got breathless and grabby, he curled his fingers into the back of her hair, which was now long enough to pull, and gave a tiny tug. He leaned back enough that his nose touched hers. "What's the reason?"

"For?" She didn't follow.

"Your hair." He tugged lightly again at the three-plus centimeters of length that had been previously razored to her neck for as long as he'd known her—practically a military cut in the back.

She could've laughed, just to hear they were on the same page. His question led right into the things she'd been thinking about, things they'd have to talk about if they were going to be able to have a relationship. And sudden, unexpected kisses almost as soon as they were alone.

"Short pixie is too edgy for village life. They expect a

lady hairstyle." She didn't actually make air quotes around the word, her hands were too busy holding on to him, but she eye rolled some implied air quotes to him. "Ironic since they prefer to follow a man, but if it's got to be a woman, she shouldn't have a manly cut. I was advised."

Again she made use of the eye punctuation.

"So if you don't grow your hair, they want you to sell the vineyard?"

"No one said that, but the way things are, the way I'm expected to be there? Exactly opposite to how you know me." She was still pinned to the door, and it was hard to do serious talking like that, and it could get out of hand quickly. She stopped grabbing and patted his shoulders instead. "I'll explain more, but I need to say something else first because I totally forgot I was going to say it before you kissed me. I had a plan, see?"

He grinned and leaned back, then stepped cleanly away, so they were no longer touching, and things wouldn't get out of hand. "Of course you did. So what was your plan?"

"Eat these ham sandwiches, then turn off the lights and watch the aurora through the big window."

"Is 'watch the aurora' a euphemism?" he asked, cheeky smile back.

She smiled, but pretended she didn't want to grin at him. "That was the other bit. The avoiding euphemism and innuendo-related activities. For now."

"No sex?"

"For a bit?" she requested, then crawled onto the bed to sit against the wall, and tucked her feet in atop the blankets, careful of the food. "I had a plan when I came to Antarctica, for after the people who know me to be a certain way—you and Jordan—left. And it's the reason I never invited you home with me. Why I don't feel like I know myself. I want to know who I am, and I want you to know who I am before we start tearing one another's clothes off again. Because once we start that… Like a first date. Sort of."

"Right." West stayed standing for a time, a little of his natural broodiness returning to the furrow of his brow. "Tell me the boundaries. You invited me to this wee room, and I'm supposed to sit on your bed? First date? I wouldn't, well, I mean I would've done far more than sit on your bed on our first date. But generally…boundaries?"

She shook her head in a bit of a tsk. "It's the only furniture here. You can sit on the bed." There was a pause to discuss how taking his boots and suit off would be the only civilized thing to do, lest he mess up the bedding. And that it didn't mean sex was happening.

Once he was in his thermals and sitting opposite her on the bed, he waved a hand, but looked far more relaxed. "Continue."

"It's a very long story, but the short version is I was raised to be a certain way—demure, proper, sweet, lady-like, et cetera. When I went away to school in a different country, I'd already become exceptionally frustrated and I went as far the other way as was in me to go, not thinking about what I wanted so much as what boundaries I could push that I could've never pushed in Monterrosa. I decided that was the new me, made some friends and that was established. Me and Opposite Me. Hair was one thing I could easily change while I was away. Or continue changing. I began growing it out at home. But if I keep it up, I can return home with longer hair."

"Is that what you want?" West asked, looking skeptical of her plan in a way that made her want to throw her sandwich at him.

"I have no idea what I want. But hair affects how people see you, doesn't it? If it's a bold cut, it projects strength. Long bouncy waves project femininity and grace. It's two very different images. So what I'm trying to figure out, my plan for myself, was stop making decisions according to the expectations of others."

"I see." He said one more word before taking a bite of his sandwich. "Pink, too?"

"Ophelia wore lots of pink."

West almost choked when Lia referred to herself as Ophelia. And in the third person. In five words, he understood exactly what she'd been trying to tell him about not knowing herself. And how much it dismayed her.

"What happened if you didn't do as was expected?" he asked, and then realized he might be making her think of the kind of things he didn't like to think about, and changed his question. "Or now. How does it affect things now with the vineyard? Do they call you Ophelia?"

"They call me Dona Monterrosa," she said, her eyes getting a little buggy.

"Not following."

"Lady Monterrosa," she said in English. "It's over a century since the time of titles, but if you want to understand how traditional the people are, they still call the heads of *my* family Don and Dona. And before you ask, I don't know how it makes me feel to have them call me that. Besides being responsible for their welfare."

Drastically different from his childhood. And he wanted to hide it again, the exact same feeling that had led to him hiding Charlie on a fake adventure in the US. All he wanted to do was change the subject. Turn off the lights. Watch the aurora, which might not even happen tonight. Or distract her by proving how much he had missed her... despite her rules.

"You're quiet," she said, then ate the last bite of her sandwich, her eyes still full of concern but tangled with a fair amount of wariness. "You think it's shameful to not correct them when they call me Dona?"

"No," he said, having gathered that she had trouble getting them to listen to her enough as it was, so she probably needed the built-in respect of a fake title to give her words a little more weight. "I guess I was trying to figure out how I can help you with this quest to know yourself."

Not really what he was thinking, but if he told her the truth, this would all get very personal, very fast. Her problems, while definite problems, weren't bitter and twisted. She had the kind of childhood problems that weren't so ugly they couldn't be discussed. Her problem had been parents that gave her what she wanted, but only if it came with a price tag, not support. Not time. Not love…

And that's probably where this all came from, he realized. Definitely a problem, but not as ugly as a mother who'd abandoned him at nine, expecting him to take care of his little brother, age four, and the progressively worse foster homes they'd been shuffled between because of his behavior and scheming.

"You're supposed to tell me if the things I change make me unlovable," she said softly. "And, I hope, tell me your sad secrets, too."

"I don't…" He started to say *no*, but watched her mouth thin and twist to the side. That had been her complaint, hadn't it? And he'd said he wanted to dig out the ashes around them. "My sad secrets are…bad, love."

"I know." She cleared everything else off the bed and crawled down to sit beside him, leaning to turn off the light as she did. "Know how I know?"

"Because I likened them to famous catastrophes?"

She lifted his arm and tucked in at his left side, and just the act of touching helped him push some of the bile back down that always rose in his throat when he got too close to those thoughts. He contracted his arm to pull her closer, but she didn't settle until she'd taken his right hand in hers, and weaved her fingers in between. "It was pretty indicative."

"I don't know where to begin," he whispered, because saying the words out loud felt wrong in the small dark room. "Or what might be too much. We all change as we age, and things I did…"

"If the things you did are no longer secrets, they don't hold as much power to hurt you anymore." She lowered her voice, too, and he was grateful. Painful words shouldn't ever have the strength of a full throat. Painful words whispered could still bruise, but words shouted or given force could tear out big holes.

"It's not that simple."

"It is."

He shook his head.

"You don't look in the rearview mirror because something bad happened, and you want to leave it behind. Something you said was your fault?"

"Yes."

"And you're afraid of me knowing?"

He didn't immediately answer; the more she prodded at it, the faster he felt his heart rate going. It didn't take long before she felt it, too, or heard it, with her ear against his chest.

"That's why you need to tell me. And we need to take the physical stuff slow, *o namorado*."

The endearment made him smile a little. There weren't many Portuguese words he knew; most of them were endearments that sounded beautiful from her soft lips, and comforted him somehow.

He had taught her less Gaelic, but the one she preferred came out on its own on reflex. *"Leannán sídhe."*

She released his hand and turned his chin, gentle but insistent, until he was gazing down at her in the low light. "You think I'm not going to love you? I think you don't

really love me. You say that's not true and want me to believe you, right?"

"You still don't believe me?"

"I'm…" She struggled for words, then said, "Faith is
a choice. It's your job to prove my faith. And it's my job
to prove yours. If you tell me the bad things now, and I
don't go anywhere, you don't have to be afraid of them
anymore. You can trust me. And if I change something,
a few things—if I cry when things hurt me and don't feel
like I have to hide it from the world and be strong all the
time—and you don't go anywhere, I don't have to be afraid
of that anymore, either."

He closed his eyes, suddenly very tired. "It sounds so
easy when you say it that way."

The last word uttered, he opened his eyes to look at her
again, and found her face lit in soft blue light, and both
of them turned to look out the wide bubble glass at the
blue whispers across the starry black sky, pale and ghostly
waves that stretched to brilliant, almost neon blue.

She clutched at his hand, anchoring herself to him in
that way they'd never really done outside of these aurora
sightings. In that moment, such peace settled over him
that the heart, which had been threatening to pound out of
his chest, slowed, and then slowed some more. He almost
wanted to tell her everything, to empty himself out to see
if that would make room for more of this peace.

"Where do I begin? I don't know how many moves
yet," he whispered.

She pulled her gaze from the dancing sky to look up
at him again. "Then tell me your saddest memory. I'm
not going anywhere. Watch the skies with me and we'll
let it go."

His saddest memory. He didn't have to think to know
what that was, and he could tell her that. He didn't have it
in him to say those words yet. To tell her it was his fault

Charlie was gone. But he could tell her about that night. Even without his guilt, it would've been his saddest memory. The faster he got it out, the more time he'd have to win her back, if he did accidentally say more again than he meant to, and she found out how disgusting he could be.

Pulling her closer, in as few words as he could, while they both watched the serene seas swirling above them, he told her about a six-hour train ride north to a Scottish morgue to identify and claim his baby brother's emaciated body.

CHAPTER TWELVE

WHEN LIA HAD invited West to view the aurora in her cabin, she hadn't really intended on him sleeping there. Sleeping beside him made it harder to avoid sex. Although she knew that boundary wouldn't last long with them, she wanted to lead back into that physical intimacy more naturally, as an emotional progression, not just because it was difficult to keep their hands and mouths from taking over when they were alone. Those kinds of distractions would allow them to duck the other things they needed to do. The important emotional excavating they were doing.

He'd told her one story about his brother, just one, and it had already changed things. When he looked at her now, that confidence she always saw was just a little dimmed. Whatever he was hiding scared the devil out of him, and he hadn't told her all of it. The only way she knew how to prove to him that she wasn't going to walk away was to dig down to the bottom of whatever was eating at him, and just accept it. Whatever it was. Whatever he felt such guilt and contrition over that he'd run from her. Because that's what he'd done. Charlie had died, and West had fled to one of the world's harshest climates, and away from the bright, sunny future they'd planned.

She'd worked out before his trip to Dallas that Charlie had been the trigger, but at that time, she'd thought his decision had been about wasting time with someone you didn't really love. A life is short epiphany. But if she accepted that he loved her, and that he'd lied to her as a way of putting distance between them for a reason, his unannounced flight took on more meaning.

He'd thought he was protecting her. He'd still thought that when he left with Jordan and Zeke. Saying *sempre* to him couldn't have changed that much, could it? She hadn't made that connection yet, or figured out whatever he'd decided meant he could come back. And that was okay. Like he said, they had some time. It was enough that they were talking.

But tonight they weren't going to do any of that. No sex. No emotional excavation, at least not for him. Her own digging was obviously less painful than his, and could be done in some fun ways. She wasn't racked with guilt, she was just living a life of faux confidence to hide from the world. To protect old hurts, but not the same kind of hurts. Hers came from people telling her she wasn't good enough, and her believing them.

"Why are we dancing in the lifeboat again?" West asked, closing the secure, water- and weather-tight door behind them as Lia went about setting up speakers and her phone to play the music she'd set to download this morning.

"Because I don't know if I like to dance," she answered. "Well, I know I say I don't like to dance, and I know that I'm a terrible dancer, but I don't actually know if I like it. It's possible to like things that you're just terrible at, right?"

"I suppose." He shrugged, but he'd taken part in scheduling their deep dives, as well, and he knew this was a no-torture zone. He wouldn't have to bare any parts of his soul tonight, unless there was some part of the soul that showed whether you could or couldn't dance.

"Help me move the furniture back." It mostly consisted of oversize ottomans pushed together in clumps to act like elevated platforms. Easy to move out of the way in all directions to make a dance floor. Even a dance floor for terrible dancers.

"Tomorrow are we going to practice kickboxing to see if you like it? Gates didn't seem to think much of it." West made a goofy face at her.

She felt her face wrinkle in dismay, remembering the strange fight between Nigel and a very angry guy called Wilson in the dining hall earlier. "I can already tell you I don't want to be punched in the face. We should probably have stuck around to ask what was going on with those two."

"It's not a medical problem until security refers them for violent behavior," he said, urging her out of the way and taking over sliding the big weird ottomans.

She wasn't sure. "I can't see Nigel being violent. Just mostly inspiring it."

"There's that." West offered her a hand in his most debonair pose once the floor had been cleared.

There were several lifeboats littering Fletcher, which weren't exactly boats, but were designed to protect those inside in the case of catastrophe. Fire being the big worry, it could grow wildly out of control in moments on the Earth's driest continent. The lifeboats had separate ventilation systems, separate power, separate heat and water and meager food supplies. Basically, large capsules that could hold and keep alive a few dozen souls until evacuations could ensue.

So maybe they were useless in the winter; Lia wasn't sure. What she did know was how very unlikely they were to be interrupted by anyone, especially two people squabbling about whatever and throwing punches, or even just throwing shade. Only West would have to suffer through her attempts to dance, and probable further attempts to *enjoy* the terrible dancing.

Once that was done, he nosed into the bag she'd also brought and pulled out a bottle of vintage Monterrosa Port proudly dated 1985. "Am I holding a small fortune here?"

"Aye, lad." She tried to Scottish at him, and then amended, "Laddie? What *do* you call a big handsome fellow?"

"You call him West—or I believe you have other special names for him." He gestured to ask if he could open it, and she gestured in return to the bag.

"I decided Monterrosa Port had probably never made it to Antarctica before, and if I was going to bring it, then I should bring one of the best vintages. Spirited it from the family cellar while packing."

"Spirited, eh? Have you already been into your cups or does dancing inspire terrible puns in ya?"

"We haven't danced yet." But they were going to. "I brought lots of different styles of music, so we can go about this in a thorough and scientific manner. This is a research station, after all."

He poured them each a small glass of the fragrant dessert wine and took a sip. "Ye gods, why have we not drunk this before? Did you keep it back in London?"

"Not this particular vintage, but I always had a small amount."

"I might have to forgive them for making you be Ophelia if they keep making this stuff." He looked at the screen on her phone where it was mounted with the little speakers, and hit Play.

It was a good thing they'd eaten before coming, as West tackled the exercise with all the glee of a drunken Scotsman. For no less than four hours, well past a sensible hour for sleeping, they danced, or tried to. Pop. Hip-hop, where she almost blacked his eye. Waltz. Salsa. She tried to *chula*, and it looked like she was stomping on ants.

By the time they caught glimpses of strangely pink aurora through the long bank of windows along one side of the lifeboat, he'd even made a comical *forbidden dance* come-on, which was all eyebrows and swirling hips that had them both tumbling onto the nearest ottoman laughing.

But as the laughter faded, and they rested from all the graceless flailing about, she still couldn't catch her breath.

"Is it stuffy in here?" she panted, words she hadn't uttered since she'd arrived. "I need some air, and I want to see the pink aurora outside without glass in the way."

"Ophelia's aurora?" he teased, and they both went giggling like idiots again to the exit.

"I think I got to the bottom of that one question."

"Do you like pink?"

"I do."

"Me, too. Especially when it's got a bit of a warm brown tone to it."

She almost laughed again; the fool was making nipple jokes. "I heard that about you."

He grabbed the handle for the door, gave it a twist and a jerk, and nothing happened. He tried again, then bent to examine the handle. Instantly, the laughter stopped.

"It's locked?"

He felt around with his fingertips, and then gave it another twist, then pulled up on it as hard as he could. "Don't see a lock on it."

"Panel," she said as soon as she noticed the very small electronic screen on the far side of the frame. She tapped it, but it didn't come on. Then employing West's method of fixing the broken door, she slapped around at it a few times, then looked for other buttons.

"Not working, either?" he asked, and she realized it wasn't just her. He was breathing as fast as she was. He stepped up behind her to eye it over her shoulder. "No buttons."

"Nope. Looks like a dead smartphone, but no side button to reboot."

"You brought your radio?" he asked, and they both turned to look at the counter where the phone sat with speakers broadcasting country music, because they hadn't gotten to the line-dancing portion of her experiment. Beside the port and the phone sat her radio.

"I'll call someone…" She glanced at her watch, frowned and hurried over to make the call. "Maintenance is on call all the time, too, right? Like for emergencies?"

"Far as I know. Someone should have a radio, even if it's after midnight now."

About ten minutes later, now fully aware the reason the door didn't open and the panel was not powered up, they stood on the other side of it, listening to men working on the outside, trying to fix the electronics.

"This is kind of a bad design, if it locks people in and suffocates them. How many ventilation issues could they have?" Air issue. And it was getting colder, probably because they'd stopped their hours-long thrashing about in the most rhythmic manner Lia could muster.

"I don't know. They said that things got switched around from the original plan when they changed up the parts open and closed for the winter," Lia said, and he could see that she was back to trying to be stoic, but the only light in the room came through the bank of windows, casting everything pink. "Let's just go sit and watch the aurora through the window. They'll get this open, but we're using more air standing around than if we went to sit."

With all their things stashed in the bag she'd carried in, and no more country music or death metal, they took a seat on the ottoman that had landed below the windows, and he kept one of her hands in his while she gripped her radio with the other.

Another twenty minutes in, West became fully aware of how little oxygen he was getting when his vision started to darken at the edges. He looked over to see Lia with her chin to her chest, and the radio now only resting in her lax hand.

"No! Lia, open your eyes," he barked at her, then shook her shoulders until she did as commanded. "We're going to get out, okay? Right now."

"The door?"

"No, baby, we're going out these windows." It took far too much effort to pick himself up from the ottoman where they'd been lounging, but he managed to move one down so when the window shattered, it wouldn't get on her. All he needed was a weapon.

He looked around in the low light and saw nothing he could swing. No stools. There was a table. Could he break a leg off?

Keep on going became his mantra in those minutes, especially when he looked at Lia and found her unconscious again.

He flipped the table over, examined the construction, then cursed it. No-breaking molded steel. What else? What else?

The bottle.

He took a big swig for luck, then smashed the bottom against the table, knocking it off and making a nice, jagged weapon out of it.

The crash made her open her eyes again, but they were so bleary he wasn't even sure she'd really awakened.

"You wanted to know how many times I've moved? Right? Wake up. I'll tell you." He climbed into the tall windowsill above her and began using the broken end of her port bottle to dig at the seal wrapping around the Plexiglas windowpane. "As a kid I moved three or four times per year between foster homes."

"Foster homes?" she repeated, her voice small, and she looked really out of it, like her eyes wouldn't focus and she was trying hard to keep them open.

"Yes. And they sucked."

"All of them?"

"Yes. I didn't want Charlie in them, or they didn't want us." He looked over, breathing heavily, to see her head drooping forward. "Lia!"

Nothing. He got hold of the long strip of seal and pulled, opening up a tiny gap around the window frame. Cold air pushed right into the space. He got two breaths, then shouted, "Ophelia Monterrosa!"

He jumped down to pick her up and hold her face by the air gap. In about thirty seconds, she'd regained consciousness.

"Stay there," he said, climbing back into the frame to dig out another strip of the rubbery sealant, and rip that down the seam. It didn't tear evenly. Sometimes it just started stretching, then tore, but when it did, he'd use his broken bottle to dig out another handhold. "My rubbish childhood is going to get us out of here, though. Using the skills learned there."

"You learned to break into places?"

"No, though I could've done if I felt it necessary." He got out one entire side, and then jumped down to do the bottom edge. "I discovered that if I broke things, they moved us. We're getting out because I was a bad kid who could figure out how to break anything. And if I break two seams on this window, to the corner, we'll be able to pull it out of the frame."

"Why did you break things?" she asked, still not keeping up, still not functioning on all cylinders.

"Because the next place could be better. For me. For Charlie."

He'd never admitted that before, denied it through all the times that he was rightly accused of it.

"We're going to need the men to come around and push it in for us. Call them on the radio."

She had to move away from the fresh air crack to get to the radio, and with her oxygen levels so depleted, she began to droop and slur her words much quicker than she previously had.

He dragged her back to the corner, which he'd freed, and they both sat, faces to the crack, watching flashlights bobbing their direction through the dark. Soon, four men stood outside the glass, and through a series of gestures and West pulling Lia the hell out of the way, the glass soon bent inward, and the sound of the rest of the remaining rubber sealant ripping almost drowned out the hissing of exceptionally cold wind entering the lifeboat.

"You know that door saying?" she asked, coherency returning. "About God shutting doors?"

"He opens a window?" he asked, and when he looked over, he found her smiling at him and pointing.

"Pretty sure that was me. And those lads with the torches."

They took a moment and just breathed, leaning into one another, and when she looked steady enough and like she was getting too cold, West grabbed her bag, slung it over his shoulder and helped her climb through the window to their rescuers.

Half walking, half stumbling through the snow, they reached an entry port, and made their way inside to warm air, then the clinic, and finally the hospital, and sat together, each with cannula of oxygen running across their noses.

"I'm feeling a little better," Lia mumbled when she saw

how intently he watched her. "But I know we said no sleep-ing in the same room…for a while…"

"I'm sleeping in your cabin tonight. Don't even try to send me to mine." He meant it to sound kind of like a joke, but it didn't come out that way, too many what-ifs in his head.

What if she'd died just when he was getting her back?

What if he hadn't come back when he had?

"We need to tell the captain to have the other lifeboats tested. Pretty sure this one is out of commission until sum-mer when they can replace the window."

"They can put the glass back in and do another seal if they get on it tomorrow. Otherwise, it might fill with snow."

"Hey," she said, sharply enough to draw his immediate attention, and she pointed at his hands, which were still fisted and white across the knuckles in his lap. "What are you thinking of?"

"Nothing good."

"Tell me."

"I was thinking that if I had stayed gone, no one would've gone to the lifeboat to dance tonight and got-ten trapped."

"Regretting coming back?"

"No. But the problem might not have been discovered until it was critical if you hadn't wanted to go dance ter-ribly there." He tried to explain. "If people had gone there in an actual emergency, that boat could've become a tomb. People who are in this part of the station, near the clinic. You."

"It's good you came back. Why is that making you want to punch something?"

"I don't. Just…having a hard time shaking it off. I'm tense all over." He leaned down to the nurse on the stick, grabbed the pulse oximeter and slipped it onto her finger.

When they'd arrived, her blood oxygen was very low, but with a few minutes of the good stuff, it was once again in the high nineties. Soon to be better.

"Would a hug help?" she asked, voice sweet and arms open.

He didn't wait for her to ask again, and didn't wait for her to come to him. He slid off the trauma table and stepped between her legs to pull her against him. She wrapped her arms around his shoulders, and looped her legs around his thighs, then laid her cheek on his shoulder.

Warm, soft and alive in his arms… He felt the tension begin to ebb away, enough for him to admit, "I'm wondering how many people have been hurt by me leaving to have another fresh start."

He knew of one, but he wasn't ready to tell her he'd caused Charlie's in every way but by his own hands. Not yet, but even he could see that was where this was all leading. Like a bomb that ticked without a countdown clock. He knew it was going to go off, he just didn't know when.

"He's not answering," Lia called from inside her office, listening to the phone at the BAT on at least the twentieth ring.

"I thought you two were travel pals." He poked his head in, and though the teasing was there, neither of them really had the energy to mirror last night's playful idiocy before they almost died in the lifeboat. Never mind the day was made longer still by security ordering they give the dining hall brawlers a blood test to make sure tempers hadn't risen due to hormonal fluctuations.

She'd asked West to go to Nigel, since Angry Guy was probably in his cabin and that didn't involve going outside to reach him.

They should've been off the clock at this hour, settling

in to sky-watch from her cabin, where there was plenty of oxygen and the big bubble window.

Her email chirped just as West came into the office, and she shook her head, hanging it up. "Two minutes of ringing…he's not going to answer. Probably has his nose stuck in some galaxy or other. Told you he was going to be difficult once nighttime rolled around."

"That you did," he said. "Give it five and call again, then I just go up."

She nodded, then looked at her phone, and the speculation about Gates's problematic behavior immediately turned serious.

"What is it?"

"Email from that hospital my father was admitted to. They released his records. We only had to get an attorney involved and email a ton of documents, but…"

He moved to stand behind her and she felt his hand on her shoulder as she opened the document.

"In Spanish?"

"Well, yes."

"Can you read it?"

"It's close enough…"

He couldn't read it, though he might recognize a few words here and there. She babbled through different vitals and doctor's notes.

"You're going to have to translate before my curiosity kills us both."

"I feel like I'm looking at test results from someone who's here. Angry Guy, or Nigel," she said, then pointed to one word. "He's hypothyroid…" She scrolled back. "Damn it, Pai."

"More, Lia. What else?"

"Immature red blood cells. White cells skewing low."

"Platelets?"

"Low." She sighed again, and West's question about the fire suddenly came back to her. "How did you know?"

"That he's alcoholic?"

She nodded.

"I didn't. But your family owns a vineyard—it's not much of a stretch. With Charlie…" He stopped, sighing as if it was an act of will to say anything about his brother, or just exhausted him. But he was doing it, either to live up to his end of the bargain, or because he wanted to help. "The more he used, the more trouble he got into. After the fire, even though I know you said it was an accident—"

"It was carelessness," she cut in, dropping her phone onto the desktop. "He was on the veranda during the dry season, smoking, and tossed a used, still-burning cigarette into the garden behind."

"I thought it started in the fields?"

"No, it mostly *destroyed* fields. The people in the village, the firefighters, the farm workers, everyone helped save the manor first. The buildings. The winery. The fire ate the other direction, through the oldest Monterrosa vines. They're now mostly gone. Some were saved, but I don't know how long it'll take for them to propagate back. Even with lots of help. Which is why things are precarious. The Monterrosa grapes make the port. If we don't have them, we don't have Monterrosa port. We just have port. Douro River port, and sure that's great, but all the stores we currently have will probably become immensely valuable if we can never make any the same."

"That's the problem with the vineyard? I thought it was just reconstruction and the old guys not wanting to listen to you…"

"The cellars where it's aging are fine. We didn't lose any product, so we have several years of sales ahead of us. But then we have a looming dry season that will span however long it takes us to replant."

"Aw, hell, love."

"Making more sense why I have to live there and run the vineyard now?"

"If you've all those people counting on you," West said. Normally, he'd have been put out that her personal family calamity might be changing the future from what they'd planned and dreamed up, but at that moment, he didn't want to consider what would come after they'd left Fletcher. Eight months was a long time.

To smooth that over, he said, "If it makes you feel better, that might not have been a drunken mistake. Judging by the tests, carelessness and inattention are probable symptoms. Mental impairment comes with low thyroid."

"I guess," she whispered, slumping a little in her seat. "He was admitted for that. Thrown out of a bar for fighting. Can you imagine? A sixty-three-year-old man, in a bar fight, and belligerent with police? They brought him to the hospital once they found out who he was."

"Not arrested?" Wealth had privileges.

She shook her head. "This behavior might be a little more exaggerated than usual, but it's still *him*. It doesn't surprise me. But this thyroid business does."

"You didn't know about the alcoholism, either," he reminded her.

"No." She sighed. "Maybe it's just shock. I wasn't expecting this. I was expecting something injury related, not…pathology."

He made a mental note to keep a sharp eye on her thyroid levels as another thought occurred to him. "You said you might have a grandparent with thyroid issues."

And now he wasn't just her jerkish father who messed things up and dropped off the face of the planet. He was her jerkish father who did all those things maybe because he was sick. And she was a doctor, and she hadn't paid enough attention to him to notice.

"No other word about where he is?"

"No. His mental capacity is strong enough to keep ahead of us, the way he's making withdrawals just before he leaves somewhere."

"What have you tried?"

"Investigators, contacting friends, family, acquaintances, staking out favorite places, sending frequent emails, sending regular paper mail to his flat in Lisbon, sending people by, paying off the doorman. You know, the usual. Everything I can legally do."

She was dancing all around it, and he'd heard twice now that her father withdrew money from the bank before he left somewhere. She might be able to freeze that account, providing it was a family account, but she was smart; she'd have thought of that.

He gestured for her to come to him, and opened his arms. It took one second for her to catch on, and she stood and leaned against him, arms circling his waist as he brought his around her.

Freezing the account would find him, but it came with risk. The same kind of risk he took when he drew the final line in the sand for Charlie. Tough love…

He squeezed her tighter and tilted his head to nose her pink knit cap.

"Anything we're missing?" she asked, turning her nose to his neck, and anything he might have thought to say would've been gone, anyway.

"Sounds like you're doing what you can."

"It helps, just talking about it." She squeezed. "Feels better."

It didn't solve anything, talking…but he said what he was supposed to say. "Good."

"Want to help some more?"

"Sure?"

"Stay with me tonight? I want to talk to you about something else with the vineyard. Something I've been mulling over."

"Yeah…" He let go, kissed her cheek and stepped back. "Then I'd better go drag Gates out of the BAT for blood work."

"I'll get Angry Guy."

"Does Angry Guy have a name?"

"Wilson, I think," she answered, then picked up the supplies she'd already prepared to go do it. "Call when you get there."

"Why? It's not a drive across country."

"So I don't worry you've been lost in the snow."

"Take security when you see Angry Guy, so I don't worry about you being alone with someone prone to violence."

Lia's trip to see Wilson was much quicker than West's haul up the steep snowy hillside, so she got back to the clinic about five minutes before he called, one word: her name through the radio.

"You made it, I see," she answered. "Are your bits frozen off?"

"I need assistance," his voice said, all playful teasing vanishing. "Gates has been stabbed. I need a stretcher, saline, emergency triage supplies and security."

"Who stabbed him?" He'd just gotten into a fight with Angry Guy, how many enemies had he made?

"Don't know," came the quick answer, then, "Send security. Don't you come, it's not safe."

Lia snorted, and immediately disregarded that order. She did get the supplies, and two from security to accompany her, but she wasn't sitting out of this for any reason.

Twenty minutes later, with two helpers loaded with

two separate emergency surgery bags, they made the mad scrambling climb to the telescope.

All the while, her mind wouldn't stop spinning. What if the one who stabbed Nigel was still there? With West? Logically, she knew that Antarctica was a dangerous place, especially in the winter, but she didn't expect to be worried about their survival on a day-to-day basis.

Her lungs on fire, she let the security go in first, with guns to make sure it was safe, but only seconds before she went running, calling for West with what was left of her lungs.

"Over here!" His answer came immediately, from the other side of the telescope rotunda, and as soon as she got close enough, he said, "I told you—"

"You knew it wouldn't work," she said, taking in the setup. Nigel had been helped onto a long table to lie on his back, but it was all but impossible to see any details of his wound until she broke out a flashlight.

"How is he?"

"In pain," Nigel answered, breathless and struggling to keep from crying out.

"And awake," she added. "Hi. We're going to look after you. Just worry about breathing." She smiled down at him, on the off chance that it might give a tiny bit of comfort, then asked West, "Angry Guy?"

"Yes. Wilson, he said. Because he was snoring every night, keeping him awake."

Mark another one down for Polar T3. "I was just about to run those labs."

"So they know where he's at?"

"In his cabin, last I heard."

While they worked, cutting away minimal clothing so his wound could be visualized, one security officer relegated to holding the light for them while the other called down to the station and within minutes announced, "Wilson's in custody."

She didn't say anything else, just got Nigel's arm wrapped in a tourniquet so she could get a line in and hang saline. The blood flow didn't seem to be too much, but saline would help keep the volume up.

"Did you bring coagulants?"

"Yes." She shifted the contents of the bag she'd brought to drag out needed supplies, along with additional gauze for packing the wound. "Pack it as hard as you must to slow bleeding so we can get him down the hill."

"Did you bring a sled?" Nigel asked, making her smile this time. Joking. He never did that before. Maybe something to worry about, considering how uptight he had been about spending time in the telescope for his research.

"I always bring a sled with me, everywhere I go now."

In about ten minutes, they had him stabilized and strapped to the stretcher, then out of the BAT and on the stairs back down.

Although she was the physician on duty for these situations, Nigel was West's patient. They got him into Medical and she fell into step behind him, ready to assist as he had assisted her with Eileen's fan-blade accident.

Unlike that night, they needed blood tonight. "I'll get the files and get his match in."

"Sedate first. It'll slow his heart."

"Slow my heart?"

"That's good, Nigel," Lia explained while digging the appropriate medication out of the cabinet and getting it loaded up to dispense into his IV. "It means you're not pumping as much blood, and less of it is leaking out. You have any allergies I need to know about?"

"No..."

"Don't worry, we're going to take good care of you. Okay?"

He nodded, and she slipped the needle of the syringe into the port on the IV to put him to sleep. "See you in a minute, Space Man."

Or a few hours, but sedation would make it only seem like a moment once he woke.

West cut off Nigel's jacket and shirts, but got the rest of it off without destroying anything. Lia checked his file for blood information, the notes she'd made about who he cross-referenced with, and called two of the crew for impromptu donations.

"How bad is it?" she asked, rejoining him after making the calls and getting ready to help.

"Not enough blood on the outside, considering his pressure. It's going somewhere."

"We should get a CBC before getting started, if he's more or less stable, and we're waiting for his donors," she suggested. West went with it, getting the blood kit he'd taken with him to the telescope to do a draw as she ducked back out to set up the donors with chairs and needles as soon as they arrived.

They alternated watching over the patient while the intervening tests were done and two donated pints of blood collected.

Once West was certain he wouldn't immediately bleed out, they prepped him for surgery.

Both of them scrubbed in, and once they were certain his anesthesia had fully taken hold, West opened the wound further to see what damage had been done and repair it.

"Spleen?" she asked, once he'd stopped cutting.

"Nicked it. I need more light."

She tilted a ring light to the wound, then got a wand to suction out the blood pooling in the abdominal cavity.

"I think it's stopped bleeding… Very small nick."

Again he was struck by what could've happened with her there alone, without another doctor there. Over snoring.

"We need to do weekly thyroid checks, and maybe start a log where everyone marks down how much they're sleeping per night. Before any of this gets further out of hand," she grumbled, handing him whatever he needed before he needed it.

"You know, it's not endemic. It's this one fight that's been repeating."

"I heard tales of overwinter syndrome when I got here. I just thought it was exaggerated."

Spacey was what he'd been seeing, but the mood swings? Part of him wanted to grab her and run to the nearest boat home—it was bad enough that the station was trying to kill them, now there were people getting in on the action.

His only comfort was that this time when the urge came to run, at least it was to run *with* someone, not away from them.

CHAPTER THIRTEEN

IN THE WEEK that passed since Nigel had been stabbed, Lia had learned to treasure short moments where she and West could steal a kiss, or the half an hour window after someone had checked on their one inpatient, the stabbed astrophysicist. In those brief periods, they would sneak into her cabin and sit on the bed to watch the night sky for streaks of color, whatever shades they may be, and talk.

That was their time, between the chaos of two doctors monitoring one patient around the clock. Moments between when he left her bed, where he'd slept alone, and she crawled into the sheets that still smelled of him later.

But today Nigel had been discharged to sleep in his own cabin, and his now-contrite and formerly stabby neighbor, now on thyroid therapy, had been moved to a bunk in the security office until they could figure out what to do with him. Barring emergency, it was Lia and West's first night together since the one where they'd nearly died in the lifeboat.

They'd had dinner, talked about work, then retired to her cabin to change into sleep clothes and curl up on the bed together, her back to his chest and his arms around her, bearded chin on her shoulder, watching the sky. It took a clear sky to see the aurora, and it was a little overcast, which led to other thoughts brewing.

It wasn't long before West's low voice rumbled in her

ear. "We haven' talked about whether we're still in the 'no good touching' zone."

She knew that timbre in his voice. Teasing, playful, definitely hoping to stir something up.

And she couldn't resist him in this mood. She twisted to meet his gaze, adopting her best fake scowl. "Are you saying my touches have been bad?"

"Oh, no," he denied quickly, pressing a quick little kiss to her mouth. "Your touches are always good. I imagine. I almost remember them."

"We might need to check your thyroid levels," she tsked, because she was nowhere near as good at the playful she-nanigans as he was. "Because of forgetfulness. You got that, right? The forgetfulness part of low thyroid?"

When he laughed, she laughed with him.

"If you have to explain the joke…"

"Yeah, yeah," she groaned, but shrugged. She had to play along. There was no choice to be had. It made her smile too much, even if it was quite literally the only dance she was good at—what came next, not this clumsy verbal tango he exceeded in. "I've got nothing."

"Got me."

Just hearing those two words made every cell in her body smile, but going gushy wasn't how the game was played.

She lifted an eyebrow at him.

He lifted one in return.

Then both brows.

Then wiggled them and graced her with such a cheeky grin she had to laugh at the fool.

With her off her game, he turned her to face him just as he rolled to meet her. The bed wasn't big, and rolling involved a bit of scooting and adjusting, but soon, he had one leg between her furry pink legs and his arms around her, their noses nearly touching as he stared down, looking happy, relaxed, charming as the devil.

Just looking, up close and personal, in a way that demanded attention and fully gave his own. He stole a little kiss, and then another. Almost chaste, were it not for the full-body contact happening.

"You could charm the starched white panties off a nun, you know that?"

"Never tried." He shifted to one elbow so he could pull her hat off, then did his. "I think I like the new hair. It's out of control. Feels right for Antarctica. Have you decided if you like it?"

"Oh, I hate it," she admitted, then shrugged. "But I think I might like it in the future. When it's a little longer and I don't feel like I'm going to be accused of time-traveling from the 1980s. I've been fantasizing about having a ponytail on hot days, and not having to fix it every day."

"It's *haircuts* you're fantasizing about?" He sounded so outraged she laughed again.

"In my defense, when you get a supershort pixie, you think it won't need work to make it look right, but it's tons. You have to blow it dry every single day."

"Or wear a hat."

"Or wear a hat!" she echoed with a grin she felt in her bones, then she slid her hands up his back, just to feel him, up and down the flexed muscles along his spine. "Which you removed."

"I could help you out of those terribly sexy, fuzzy pajamas, too. I mean, if you wanted."

She made like she was considering it, then shook her head. It only took a little pressure from her hands sliding to his chest for him to ease onto his back.

"You undressing me would not provide any surprises. Instead, you've been in Antarctica on the insane metabolism diet for months, grown this manly beard. I'm curious to see if you've sprouted impressive fur elsewhere. In the name of science, I must do research!"

This time it was him laughing. He splayed his hands, palms forward, to show them off. "You should probably look here for hair. I heard that sometimes it's a problem when a lady puts her man in the 'no good touching' zone and he must 'good touch' himself."

She laughed again. "Well, if you pass inspection, the ban might be lifted. But I'm going to have to get this shirt off you. And the pants. Everything must go. My medical integrity is on the line."

"Can't have that, can we?"

The way he watched her was some heady mix of desire, amusement and contentment, and made it impossible for her to go as slowly as she wanted.

She rid him of his top, and then froze as she saw her ring on the chain around his neck. He looked at her for a moment, and the chance this evening could turn upside down suddenly sat between them.

Not what she wanted. It wasn't time to talk about the ring. And she could see the clasp. Gingerly, she pinched the little claw and removed the chain from his neck, placed it onto the bedside table and turned her attention to his drawers with the same kind of popping eyebrow wiggle he'd given her.

Just like that, the tension passed. She was free to go as slowly as she wanted, draw out the moments that somehow felt new. He helped wrestle his thermal layers off, then unzipped her ridiculous onesie to find three layers of thermals beneath.

"You're like one of those Russian dolls." He didn't stop to count layers, just burrowed his fingers beneath all the waistbands he could find and, once he hit skin, pulled them off, knocking her socks off in the process.

"I'm built for a more temperate climate. You're going to have to keep me warm."

Stretching out beneath the blankets, he pulled her again half under him, and made his intentions clear with the kind of kiss that could turn her inside out. One kiss, and then another, all thought of playing doctor gone in the moment. Kissing until breathless, just to stop again so he could look at her, at her hair, her face, into her eyes.

His arm supported her head, fingers twined with her hand curled there, and just looked. Nose to nose, his warm breath fanned her cheeks, eyes just locked to hers for long, intimate stretches of time. She couldn't even say how long, just long enough that she had to know what was going on in his head. She wanted complete connection, not just hands, eyes and skin molding together.

"Are you telling yourself a story for the future?" she asked, because that's what he did. He dreamed of the future, built castles in the air, and had invited her into them.

"No," he said softly, his eyes crinkling at the corners as he smiled. "I'm right here. With you. Right now. One hundred percent."

She had to swallow a sudden thickness in her throat, his answer cutting through the need to name what she felt, to know if he felt it, too. He did.

It was different this time. They were different. All the times they'd touched and loved had been different. Had been less, somehow, even if she hadn't known it in those moments.

Passionate, desperate, hungry, playful, flirty, but this… connection. And he wasn't even inside her yet.

Hand free, she slid it down his chest, ruffling at the crisp male hair dusting his chest and belly, all pretext of a fur inspection gone as soon as she reached the hard length of him pressed at her belly, and she stroked her fingers over the wet head, making his breath stop, then stutter.

One little touch and he let go of her hand so he could free his arm and slide over, center himself above her.

She pointed to the bedside table where she'd already made a small tear in the condom packet she'd placed there.

No words passed; he simply covered himself, gripped his erection to ease through her slick folds, then slowly slid inside her. Several months had passed since they'd last been together, but it had never been like this. They'd never had this searing connection that made him go so achingly slow, eyes still locked to hers. Still there, with her, one hundred percent.

They'd been that couple who would annoy everyone with sneaky kisses and flirting, and the lighthearted, playful, energetic coupling of the first months of their relationship had barely deepened. Until life had torpedoed them. And she'd made sure it had been devastating.

And it all could've been avoided, if she'd been unafraid to tell him the truth about what was going on in her head, why going home was so hard for her. Why she didn't want him to witness it, or how weak she knew she'd appear to him there. If she'd asked him to come with her, for support, she'd have been there when he needed her, too.

Would he have accepted her then? Without months and a painful separation? Without life breaking down their barriers? Maybe. Maybe not. But he'd deserved the truth.

"I'm sorry." She whispered the words, feeling her eyes dampen, and he stilled, the love in his eyes so completely undisguised even she could see it.

"Why are you sorry?"

"I'm sorry I didn't trust you and explain that last day in London." She sniffed and stilled as he kissed away the tears trickling from the corner of one eye. "I'm sorry I didn't trust you would still love me."

"You did," he reminded her softly, still holding himself

perfectly still and hard within her. "You came all the way to Antarctica for a reason, love."

"Yeah…"

"Maybe we're just slow learners." He smiled then, a tender, soft curl of his lips, then leaned in and kissed her. Long, slow and deep, a kiss that bordered on worshipful. When he began to move again, she couldn't stop the stuttering, gasping sounds he wrung out of her.

Under the glorious thickness of him, the friction and depths built slowly, until she felt it scratching down her spine, and spiking the arches of her feet. He held her there until she couldn't take one more second, then picked up the pace. Faster. Deeper. Until the world went white and that desperate, clawing pleasure sang through her. But more, it wasn't just pleasure he gave in that moment, staring into his eyes, feeling him quaking inside her; it was more than that future they'd planned and promised. It was them, truly who they were, without armor, sharing the pieces of their hearts that had been hidden and protected for so long. The parts of their souls that had never been allowed to join before.

After, when he'd rolled with her in the narrow bed to anchor her to his side, his chest rapidly rising and falling beneath her cheek, she knew he'd felt it, too. It was in his long, trembling fingers continually petting her hair back from her forehead, and the other hand that twined with hers.

And the silence. No quips, no teasing, no joking boasts about his exceptional performance, just holding, touching, until hearts slowed. Until she lifted her face to look at him again, and noticed the pink cast of the room, the pink light.

He lifted his chin purposefully toward the bubble window, and she tilted her head back down to look out.

The dazzling light show could've just started, or it

could've been going on as long as they had. Pink and blue in alternating waves, purple where they overlapped.

Beauty, peace and contentment. She watched until his hand stilled, and his breathing turned slow and deep, then turned to watch him instead, the soft light playing over his handsome features, relaxed in sleep, until she followed him.

West woke sometime later, the two of them curled together in the small bed, nose at the back of her neck, and the unruly brown hair she currently hated, but which made him smile, tickling his face.

She shifted and he tightened his arms around her and murmured in her ear, "Don't go squirmin' unless you're lookin' to wake the beast."

Her soft laugh and purposeful bum wiggle was sexy and adorable in one go.

"Unless that's your wish, then I'm sure I can oblige."

"Well, I would absolutely—" she paused, looking over her shoulder at him "—but after, can we talk about the vineyard first? I meant to do that earlier."

Talk about the vineyard? He tried not to groan, he really did, but his throat did what it did.

"It's not a bad thing. I just want your opinion on something. I woke up a while ago, and I've been thinking to the dancing sky and the music of soft snores in my ear."

He grinned, even if she couldn't see it, and gave her a good squeeze. "Right, then, talk fast. Get it done before I let the lad have his way."

She squirmed and made to roll over, so he loosened his arms to accommodate her, and soon had one shapely leg wrapped over his hips, and a tangle of arms together.

"Traditional village, right?" she said.

"*Sim*, Dona Monterrosa."

His meager Portuguese earned him a grin, but she kept

on with her deep thinking. "Things are not that much different than they were a century ago. They didn't get electricity until the 1960s, so it's been very slow adapting to modern ways," she murmured, with a touch of dismay clinging to her tone. "I want to bring them more into the twenty-first century…"

"How? Broadband?"

"Don't laugh. I actually got that done when I first went back."

"For real?"

She nodded. "Wasn't dial-up before, but it did run over phone lines and was hideously slow. Also pulled some strings and got a new cell tower installed closer for more reliable service."

"Impressive."

"The cell tower was an easy decision. What I'm considering isn't so clear-cut."

She sounded uncertain, and he was starting to see that anything to do with the vineyard and the village was where she was most uncertain in her life. That and her father, but he wasn't really in the picture now. She might not think she knew herself, but it seemed to him that it was more that she didn't know how to fit into what they wanted her to be.

The way she lay there, with the lights returned to the skies, the pink hue colored her dusty pink nipples, which stood from the chill in the air.

The urge to interrupt her with his mouth nearly overwhelmed all sense, but she touched his arm and helped him refocus.

"What do you want to do?"

"I've been thinking about giving forty-nine percent of Monterrosa Wine to the villagers. Profit-sharing. Giving them more of a voice in the company and bringing the families in more economically as they all work hard to help us recover."

He blinked, scrambling mentally to pay a lot more attention to what she was saying. "You want to give away almost half of your company?"

"Well—" she nodded, but it was still an uncertain kind of rolling head jiggle "—I'd keep controlling interest, which would allow me to overrule any bad decisions they might not fully understand the ramifications of. Keep the company on steady ground while they get to know more of the business. Selling wine is different from making wine. Or growing grapes…"

"That's…" West didn't know what it was. Brave? Generous? Foolish? *A risk to her future security.* "Are you allowed, legally, to do that?"

"Pai only had to be gone for ninety days with proof that he was alive but neglecting duties. Then it became mine. One hundred percent. Abdication of duty clause."

"I see." Her voice said she was already certain it was what she wanted to do, but there again, maybe looking for permission? And that was something he couldn't help her decide. All he could do was try and gather more information. "Are you doing it to get away from the business and back to medicine?"

She tilted her head, brows bunching up. "I haven't left medicine. I plan on practicing part-time in the village. But I have to do something for them. They're too much in the past, and while that can be good in some ways, in others it's bad. The population is aging and the younger people move away, to one of the cities, to find opportunity. If the families have a financial stake, there is incentive to stay."

"I see…"

"You see?" she repeated, and then sat up to turn on the bedside light, a deep frown creasing the corners of her mouth. "You don't think I should do it?"

It wasn't exactly an accusation, but there was some measure of alarm in her voice.

"I don't know." He waved a hand, trying to make sure she didn't read too much into his commentary. "It's yours, your...you know, ancestral inheritance, or whatever you want to call it."

And he didn't want to muck that up. She had to know that.

"But you can have an opinion."

He sat up, too; the sexy feeling that had been wafting over him dissipated too fast to even picture trying to recover. "You don't need my opinion. You have people to consult with."

"No, I don't. Not about this." The pleading in her voice made his shoulders stiffen, alarm bells starting to sound. "I'm flying half-blind on this part of my life, and I can't exactly ask the people if they think I should do this. They would say *yes* regardless. And I value your opinion. Is that something that you would've wanted? Something that would've helped your family when you were little?"

The conversation turned, and so did his stomach. "No, but other families probably."

"But...before foster care?"

"Before foster care, it was just me, Mum and Charlie. And she didn't work in a factory or anything like that."

Her voice lost some of the shrill notes. "What happened there? Did she die?"

"She's still alive, love. She just was a bad mum, and the government came in, took us. And she never cared to try and get us back. For about six months, when she would sometimes visit, she'd tell us that was the plan, and what she was working on, but then she gave up custody. She wasn't one of those parents who struggle to give their children better lives."

When he looked back at her, she looked stricken, and almost frozen there. "I don't know what to say."

"About?"

"You don't like sympathy."

"Not so much," he admitted, then stood up, needing to move, muscles across his shoulders starting to stiffen again. "And I don't like giving my opinion on this, something this big and important to your future."

She didn't stand, too, but she did look up at him, confused, arguing in the dark. "Just tell me your first thought?"

"My first thought is, this is *your* future. I can't make decisions about *your* future."

"My future?" she said, and a little edge of frustration crept into her voice, dampening the worry.

"Your future."

"Do you still see us trying to have a family, vows, rings?" She reached over to pick up the ring on the chain from the bedside table and held it up to him, her sweet face stuck somewhere between scowling and those seconds before someone cried, when the domino was about to fall.

They hadn't spoken about a new engagement, hadn't had enough time to talk about much of anything this week. He took the chain and slung it over his head. "Let's just take a breath. I'm not saying no future together. That's nothing to do with this."

"Of course it is. The vineyard is your future, too, if we're together."

"And you'll still be running it." He looked around for his thermals, and pulled the pants on. "The men will get used to having a woman for a boss, and start listening without so much effort. Isn't that the whole point of modernizing it?"

"No," she said, and was full-on scowling now. "I'm not talking about the vineyard anymore. I'm talking about how you keep doing this. You give diagnoses on my father, but no opinions about how to deal with him. You don't give them about the vineyard, either. You have opinions—I see them running all over your face—but you won't share them with me. I love that we're talking about our lives and we're both trying to be open and grow together. Lean on each other. And when we were together…it was different. It was more. We're *more* than we were. Why don't you want to take part in that future? Do you not want it?"

"If you want to do it, you should do it," he said again, but he was already half-dressed, ready to make his escape. But first give her a minute to calm down.

"I can be strong. I can be the strongest person in the world, but I don't want to have to be that person all the time. We're great partners, we work together so well, and we can play and have fun and have…tonight. We—" She stopped, words obviously failing her when she tried to describe what had happened tonight. Which had definitely been more. A kind of more he didn't have words for, either, and which suddenly seemed fragile and transitory when earlier it had felt like peace. "But I want us to be partners in everything. I value your opinion. Just tell me what you're thinking."

She scampered in between him and the door, still fully naked. And cold. Her eyes locked to his, and her hands flattened against the door, like her palms touching the wood would add just enough weight to make it immovable.

Just tell her?

"Okay, fine. When I came back, I made a deal with myself that I would only be able to be with you if I was putting your safety ahead of my own. Your life is more valuable. That was my deal with myself. Physical safety. I can't make decisions about your future, or about your family, for you. My job is to keep you from harm."

"Why?"

"I don't even know if we'll make it once we get past the winter. Maybe we'll both go screaming the other direction once we set foot back on soil instead of snow."

"What happened?" she asked, then grabbed his cheeks to keep him looking her in the eye. "I know this is about

Charlie. I know that he died. You told me you never loved me to keep me away from you, didn't you? And you said that the catastrophes in your rear view are your fault. Is that what this is about? What happened to him?"

"He overdosed."

"Did you shoot him up?"

"No. But I might as well have. Okay?" The question was like battery acid in his mouth, and his reaction was just that, words said by reflex, at least at first. "He didn't overdose by accident. And he did it right after I went to tell him that he couldn't be a part of our family unless he got help. Because I couldn't risk you, or our future family, exposing them to an addict who was erratic enough to be dangerous. Get clean or get out. And he…"

He stopped there, the back of his neck aching enough he felt the need to rub it away.

"You told him to get clean, or he wasn't welcome with us, and he took too much on his own?"

He nodded.

"That's not your fault."

Those words brought that ice dagger back to the base of his skull, the sharp, frigid pain he'd felt that first day he saw her.

"See? I *knew* you would say that. But it *is* my fault. I was so busy and so focused on how I wanted that conversation to go that I didn't hear what he actually said. I didn't hear him at all. I heard excuses. When he said, 'I hope you have a good life,' I heard a passive-aggressive jab. Later, when I replayed the conversation—what I could even remember of it—I realized he was saying goodbye. He even told me he loved me, and I didn't hear him. Tell me that's not my fault."

She opened her mouth, but nothing came out, just a kind of confused and near frantic waffle of her breath.

"If you still want me after this, I will stay with you forever." He crammed his feet into his boots, fully ready now to go. "There's probably very few lows I wouldn't stoop to, to keep you safe. But I make bad decisions when it comes to the emotional health of people I love. You can't ask that of me if this is going to work."

"West…"

"You want another example? You want to know what I want you to do with the vineyard?"

She looked less certain then, her eyes once more full of worry and fear, but she nodded.

"I want you to keep it. I want you to keep the whole damned thing because money means security. Sure, you're doing fine with your job, but money means security. You don't know what will happen in the future, and I don't give a damn about those sweet little cartoon people who live in the nineteenth century and probably all sing while they work, in four-part harmony, and everyone knows the words. I care about *you*. That's it."

"That's not true," she said, but it was just a processing sound. She wasn't agreeing, she was trying to figure out how to argue with him. "You care about your patients."

"For a while," he agreed, but then asked, "Your father? You want to know my opinion there?"

Again she nodded, but a touch slower. Wary.

Good.

"Cut off his access to bank funds. No company funds. He disappeared after burning down the vineyard. Press charges. He'll be found when governments get involved in tracking his passport. You want to find him? Play his game, play dirty. That's how you find him. You like my ideas?"

"I appreciate them, and—"

"Don't do that." He cut her off with one silencing jerk of his hand. "These are not decisions you would make and I cannot make them for you. I make bad decisions for other people, and they suffer for it. And then I suffer, too. See? It's not just me feeling protective. I have to protect you because if something happens to you that I should've seen coming, I won't survive it. I'll have ruined you. Taken this beautiful person and...and...maybe you end up like Charlie."

When he noticed tears starting to leak from her eyes, he dialed it back a little, and asked, "Have you changed your mind?"

"No," she squeaked. "Have you?"

It took him a second, but he nodded. "This isn't going to work. If you need someone to count on so you don't have to be so strong, or because you don't know what you want, I can't make those decisions for you. I picked you because you're strong. You wanted to know if I'd still love you if you changed? Maybe the answer is *no*. Or maybe the answer is *I love you*, but we can't make this work."

"I've already been counting on you," she whispered. "No amount of me telling you it wasn't your fault is going to help, is it?"

"A less selfish man would've heard him. That's on me. I drove him to this with a threat to take away the last person in his family. And that's on me, too."

Since she wasn't moving from in front of the door, he gently as he could took her by the shoulders and moved her out of the way.

"You can stay here. This is just a...it's a bump," she said behind him, and shifted when he gestured for her to move her nude body out of where people walking by could see in when he opened the door. "We can sort it out."

"I'm going to my cabin."

She reached a hand for him, eyes pleading. "I'm sorry you had to go through that. I'm sorry, too, that you keep trying to run from it. You can't outrun painful memories. Punishing yourself for something beyond your control isn't—"

"It's not punishing me." He was dressed; there was nothing left to do but to go, and that's exactly what he did. "It's saving you and *your* children."

CHAPTER FOURTEEN

ACID SWIRLED THROUGH West's middle, burning everything it touched, like it could eat through the very core of who he was.

He couldn't outrun it.

Now that she knew about Charlie, about how that was one long string of everything that could've gone wrong for that kid, initiated or exacerbated by West's decisions, she couldn't think he'd be okay to help with her own family problems. She had to be realizing that right now.

He closed the door on his cold, empty, tiny cabin, and dropped like lead onto the side of the bed.

The last tenant had left the shade pulled down over the wee window he had in this one, to block out the constant summer sunshine and make sleep easier. But at that moment, it made the room smaller.

Was the aurora still there? He hadn't even looked at her window before going. If he watched the aurora maybe he'd feel that peace again. Maybe he would be distracted enough not to dwell on what he'd almost had, and what he never could.

Leaning over, he rolled up the shade. The dark sky obliged his need, and he watched quietly as pink tendrils grew bolder, more intense, coming in waves from the side, like the tide washing across his window.

Pink. Which she'd realized she loved, even if it had belonged to Ophelia. But he didn't feel the peace he needed.

He'd just broken up with her, and they would be trapped at Fletcher together, in the same department, forced to work together, for the next seven and a half months. God help him, this was a mistake. Dallas would've been fine. He could've stayed in Dallas.

The pink waves broke red here and there, like warning bursts that made the back of his neck tighten and itch, and then the colors turned and wave after wave of bloody wave slithered across the night sky.

What washed over him wasn't a joyful, comforting peace; it was closer to an itch for physicality, also not the kind he preferred. He felt like prowling the corridors to keep from punching a wall.

West yanked the shade back down over his window to hide it, and flopped back onto his cold, barren bed. He unfastened the chain on his neck to slide the ring off. Something to fidget with. Something to look at other than the alarm-increasing red skies.

He slid the ring onto the middle section of his ring finger with effort, then flipped on the bedside lamp and swiveled his hand toward it to look at the thing.

Vines and flowers in three different metals, because she loved rose gold, but he liked white gold, so they added the regular gold to provide balance to the two. They braided together in a vaguely Celtic style, because the vines were her history, and the knot was his.

Flowers with tiny diamond centers dotted the vines, because grapes represent the harvest, but flowers represent the *future* harvest, what they were cultivating toward.

Everything snaked around to support the chunky perfect diamond in the center, bracketed at four corners with tiny grape leaves.

How long had it taken them to get the design to this

point to submit to a jeweler? Two months? Two and a half? A long process. Back and forth. Ideas, requests, offers, counteroffers. If it had been left to him, she would've still loved it, because that's the kind of person she was. But what had she called the ring? The physical representation of their promises for the future. Only they never could get that future going, it seemed. And he didn't even know if that was a blessing or a curse. If he should've walked out, or should've stayed. He didn't even know what was better for her anymore.

Always had brought him back, but he didn't know if he could stay, not without the confidence he would make her life better by doing so.

When he'd left Charlie, he'd been thinking of himself. Maybe he was learning. But maybe it was too late for that.

Lia slept fitfully after West's wild-eyed departure, with dreams mostly filled with meaninglessness.

Her standing in a white room, surrounded by fast-moving grapes that bounced like tiny superballs.

Her wearing a pair of shoes that judged everyone else's footwear, loudly, and for all to hear.

And the one good one, the one that felt like prophecy and instead of leaving her with a sense of frenetic, uncontrollable chaos in and around her, flowed over her like a warm, soaking bubble bath. She and West were painting a mural on the nursery wall at the manor, pink aurora on a field of purple. She didn't know how she knew it had been a nursery, but it had.

That comfort carried her through a long day without chasing him down and making him talk to her. She'd had West sightings, but zero interactions. He was grim-looking, but still functioning.

With nothing to do, she had time to think, to inventory

the clinic's supply room, and think some more. Try to sort out her West-shaped riddle.

Things could be fixed; they had to be fixable. She just wasn't sure how to go about it. She didn't even know if it was for her to fix. Seemed like the kind of thing that should be a joint effort, if they were ever going to make things work.

And she had to find a way to put them on equal footing. He'd shared the kind of information that would make anyone feel vulnerable over, but most especially someone who blamed himself for the loss of someone he'd spent most of his life protecting.

He thought he'd given her a weapon to use against him. She had to do the same for him. Get them on equal footing, show him she was still there and let him work out the rest.

She'd taken one detour to visit Eileen Gossen, who had managed to stay at the station and was healing, and enlisted her help obtaining a small part from the shop.

Now, at just after six, she stood outside the door of West's cabin, and tapped one fingernail on the wood, but with the way her hands shook, it might sound like scratching to him.

He opened the door, saw her standing there, then gestured her inside.

"I'm not sure what there is to talk about," he said, sitting on the edge of his bed, making the most of the little cabin room so it could hold two people without too much pain.

She fiddled with the small gasket Eileen had dug up for her, worrying it between her shaking fingers as she spoke.

"You don't have to talk, just listen. I'm not staying long. I just want to tell you something."

"What thing?"

"A thing I've been hiding, because I'm not going to try and pretend that we're without some issues, or that we're perfect together. I'm still sure I'll never find someone who loves me like you do. I know I won't find anyone else I love as much as you. And there's no one I trust as much as you."

"You weren't listening," he said softly, sighing as he braced his elbows on his knees.

In the cramped little room, she took one step, turned and sat on the edge of the bed beside him. "I heard every word you said, and I understand what it cost you to say it. So I'm here to do the same. And I'm here to say your words back to you. If you still want me, I'll stay with you forever. Trust you, as I trust you now. My father left me the vineyard, and it is mine right now, in a sort of temporary ownership until I marry. Then it belongs to my husband. And he had it written up that way without specifying a name, or having someone in mind. He had it written before I met you, and I just didn't find out until I was at home and he was gone."

"What?"

"When I signed the papers, that was part of it. I don't know how it would hold up in the courts, but what I do know is that it will hold up if I don't ever challenge it. And that if you were my husband, I wouldn't need to. Our children would still inherit, and it would still bear the Monterrosa name, because we'd hold to that fine Portuguese tradition of stacking names on names on names. Itamarati da Monterrosa MacIntyre. And I know you'll do whatever you can to protect me, and them."

"Love," he said, and it sounded like it took all his strength to say the word, but he'd still picked an endearment, which told her everything she needed to know. "I don't know what you want."

"I want you. And I want you to prove to yourself that you can do more than break things and hurt people you love. You broke your streak of running from people who love you when things get hard. You broke the window and got us out of the lifeboat. Now break this pattern, and trust me like I trust you."

"What do you want me to do?"

"I want you to look for a way to break my father's silence. In a way that won't hurt me, so in a way that won't really hurt him."

He looked at her strangely, but for a moment, he didn't look lost. "I don't know your father."

"But you know me," she said, then reached into her pocket to pull out a piece of paper rolled up like a scroll, with an electric blue silicone gasket wrapped around it to hold it closed. "That's his email address. He's been ignoring me."

He took it, rolled the slim blue band off the paper, and when he went to throw it in the trash, she grabbed his hand. "Eileen looked hard for that for me. Keep it safe."

"Rubber washer?"

"Gasket, a small version of what you dug out of the window for us, and I think just about the perfect size for a makeshift wedding ring. You know, if you do decide you want me still." She leaned up and pressed a quick kiss to his stunned cheek, then stood up to make her exit. "We still have about seven months to make this work. But I'm not a patient woman, so don't expect me to give up on you already."

Still using words he'd said to her, and praying they both remembered them correctly—the conversion of short- to long-term memory was harder when a brain was saturated with cortisol or oxytocin.

The next morning, knocking at her cabin door yanked Lia from sleep, her heart instantly pounding as she scrambled out of bed.

The last she remembered looking at the clock, it had been about three, hours after she'd left West, and the

amount of time it had taken for her to work through the
nerves knotting in her stomach. A glance at it now confirmed she'd gotten just about three hours of sleep. Her
radio hadn't gone off. Not an emergency.

She staggered to the door, wearing her favorite pink
pajamas, and wrenched it open.

West stood there, laptop tucked under one arm, looking tired, as she'd grown used to seeing him.

He gestured to the room, brows up and questioning. "I
have an idea."

He had an idea. The stressed awakening had popped
her heart rate up, but those four little words turned it from
a possibly scary situation, to one of hope.

She stepped back, pulling the door open wider so he
could enter, peeked past him to be sure that the clinic was
still dark, then closed the door.

Quietly, he sat on the corner of her bed, propped the
laptop on his lap and opened it. "About your father…is he
as proud of the vineyard and village, all that, as you are?"

"I seem prideful about it?" she asked, not following at
all, but unable not to frame it that way with the rest of her
chaotic thoughts about the vineyard.

"It's something you *should* be proud of. Is he? Does
he love it? Is that why he's been running, do you think?"

"Oh." She squeezed her eyes shut and then knuckled the
sleep out of them before she answered his question. "Yes.
He loves the vineyard and the history of it. He always en-
joyed the pomp—when we receive orders every year for
the same ceremonies and celebrations. He just doesn't like
the work bits. Not good at them."

Though her eyes were still gritty with sleep, she sat
beside him and waited to see if her answer aligned with
his idea.

"I know you don't approve of cutting off his access to
funds or having him arrested for arson," he began. "Too

risky. If he's not thinking straight, depriving him of money might send him off the rails. And requests haven't been working."

"Right," she said slowly, working to keep any alarm or dismay from her face or voice.

"With the caveat that I only know a few things about him, that he's a jerk to his daughter and that makes me want to punch him in the face, that he probably wouldn't mind that much since he was almost arrested for brawling in Barcelona, and that he loves his vineyard and almost burned it down, so...guilt."

She tried to keep following along, but her brain was still fritzing. "Still not following."

"I think the best chance of getting a response from him is to pick a fight about the vineyard. If it were me, I'd respond faster to a fight than a request," he said, then added, "I did actually respond to a fight when you showed up here."

She'd emailed West so many times, requesting, pleading, for him to answer, and he hadn't. She hadn't even thought to ask if he'd read her messages, or maybe had seen and deleted them, maybe blocked them. So...he had seen them, maybe even read them.

"Don't do that," he said suddenly, breaking into her thoughts. "You can yell at me later—the satellite will be here soon. Stay with me a little longer."

"I don't know his other weak points." And the idea of exploiting weak points made her uneasy, but at the same time... West was helping. Or trying. "Did you sleep last night?"

"Red aurora kept me up." He gave her a lopsided and still-half-guarded grin. "I think we know enough weaknesses to pick a fight. I think if we pick a fight with him, if *I* pick a fight with him about the vineyard, he'll answer me."

"What do you mean? What kind of fight?"

"A dirty fight." He turned the laptop around to show her an opened, unsent email. Where his fingers bent around the edge of the screen, she saw her ring crammed down as far as it would go on his ring finger, just past that first knuckle, and on that same finger sat the blue silicone gasket. He was wearing their rings, not just on a chain around his neck, hidden away.

She squeezed her eyes shut again, trying to find some focus.

"Just read it."

A deep breath, and she did as he asked.

He didn't call him names. Didn't point fingers. The email was written like a very professional letter between businessmen, stating that she had agreed with him to give up making wine. And begin making whiskey, since proper Scotch couldn't be made in Portugal. Too many of the Monterrosa grape vines had been destroyed, so they were going to plant barley, which would enable brewing to resume in one growing season instead of the years it would take for the vineyards to get back to what was needed.

It took her all the way to the bottom page where he'd included a fake logo to realize that this was just bait, not an actual proposal from him to switch production to whiskey. West had lied. Claimed a quiet elopement days ago, and that as the sole owner of the vineyard now they could make this decision without involving him. But, man-to-man, he felt he owed him a chance to convince him otherwise. And attached a deadline.

Two days, followed by the logo MacIntyre Whiskey. Not even Monterrosa Whiskey. He was going for the jugular, right in the pride centers.

"Where did you get the logo?"

"I doodled the barley with the stylus that came with the laptop, then put it on an oval, then stacked up some bigger ovals in black and white to make a frame. Picked from the fonts on the computer. It took a lot longer to make the logo than to write the inflammatory email."

"Oh." She blinked a bit at the email, then read it again, her brain still soggy with sleep. "You think he'll answer to stop us from pretend-doing this? It *is* pretend, right?"

"Of course it's pretend. I'm feeling a bit bitter that I had to smash your bottle of port to pry out the lifeboat windows. I definitely want to drink that in the future."

The future. She couldn't think about the future. Couldn't ask about it, either. It didn't mean anything that he'd done this until he said it meant something.

"Are you going to send it?"

"Not without your approval," he said, then added, "That's how we designed the ring. Do you remember?"

"We had to agree?"

"Veto power." He reached up to brush her hair back from her face, then tuck a lock behind her ear.

She nodded, somehow managed to resist tilting her head into his hand and focused on the idea still rolling around in her head. If it didn't work, did it cause any harm? Her father couldn't be angrier with her for trying anything to get him to surface.

"It's about ten minutes before the satellite passes over," he added. "Which was why I knocked to wake you up early."

What time was it in Portugal when the satellite passed over? Seven in the morning would be ten in the morning. Still morning. He'd have time to respond, and maybe even fire off an angry response immediately.

She moved the mouse to hover over the address bar, considered the email address she'd given him, then scraped her memory to come up with two more. That done, she hovered over the Send button and nodded to him to do it.

"Those are all the ones I know of. But I don't know if he's checking them."

West nodded, then picked up the laptop, clicked Send to queue it up for the instant the Wi-Fi established. "I'll let you know when he responds. If he responds."

"What if he doesn't?"

He stood up, tucked the computer under his arm again, then mashed down a spot on her crazy hair to kiss her messy crown of curls.

"Cross that bridge when it gets here. I'm ready to work, so I'll just be out there getting my schedule in order for the day, and I won't leave the department until after the sat passes out of our orbit again."

She nodded, and though he caught her looking at the ring, neither of them said a word about it, and he went out as he'd said, to get started with his day.

Reading something into either instance would make her stupid. Maybe his chain broke. Maybe he just wanted to help her so that they could work together with a little less stress for the months and months remaining of winter.

She couldn't read anything into it. He still hadn't sanctioned her plan to give part ownership of the vineyard to the village, which she was going to do. But she could wait. They had seven months, and she wasn't giving up.

The rest of the day passed at an achingly slow pace. When the satellite had passed out of range, West had made sure she saw him packing the laptop back up and carrying it out with him as he went about chasing down his physicals.

If his plan worked, she might get her father back, sort of. Or at least get to tell him he didn't have to run anymore. If it worked, it might change West's mind about whether he could do anything but damage to the lives of those he loved and not view them as one more catastrophe waiting to happen.

If it worked, she might get her fiancé back.

If it didn't? She'd be stuck waiting on Pai to come forward, or slip up so her investigators could find him. West would definitely not get over thinking he couldn't be trusted with important, life-changing decisions.

The evening satellite had come and gone, and West stopped by her cabin long enough to let her know there had been no response, looking as glum as she felt. And no longer wearing the ring.

That night, she'd visited a bar to get a couple shots of whiskey in her, in honor of their lie, like an offering to the universe for a little help. It also helped her sleep.

The last thing she remembered doing was watching an aurora-free starry sky out of her window, thinking about how someone could fall in love with the sky, and the next she knew, someone was knocking at her door.

Like yesterday, she staggered out of bed and opened it to find West standing there. This time, he didn't ask, just scooted right past her, opening the door wider and turning sideways to get into her cabin. "You overslept."

"I did?" She closed the door, then swiveled to see the clock. Five minutes past seven a.m.

Her breath caught and she turned back to West, who was grinning and opening the laptop.

"He emailed?"

He actually laughed as he spun the laptop to show her. "He's really mad."

"Did he say where he was?"

At the last second, as she almost took the computer, he pulled back. "Keep in mind, that email was designed to make him angry enough to get in my grille about this plan."

"I know." She said the words before really considering what he meant by that warning. "He's mad at me?"

"A bit." That was underplaying it; the set of his mouth

gave it away as he considered more fully how it might affect her. "Are you okay with that? You can choose not to read this, and I can give you highlights—well, the bits I can understand. His English isn't as good as yours and he resorts to Portuguese in several places."

"I've been waiting for months, I'm ready. I know we set him up to be mad." She licked her lips, rubbed her eyes again to make sure the letters would be clear and held out her hands for the laptop.

Certain phrases stuck out, and mostly they were the ones in their native tongue, the one he could most effectively jab at her in. The email was written decidedly to her, but in the form of Tell my worthless daughter...

A few familiar jabs about her being a disappointment, and how much better his life would've been if she'd been a boy. Everyone's life. Et cetera. Things designed to make her feel as badly as possible, but which had stopped having much power over her as she'd heard them so many times.

Suddenly, he took hold of the computer and pulled it right out of her hands to sit on the table. "Enough. I think you've seen enough. I'll email back..."

Suddenly, him having sent those things to West was what tipped her over the edge from mildly dismayed to actually angry.

"Oh, no," she said, snapping her fingers for him to hand it back. "I'll write to him. Because you know what? He's done way more damage to the family name than I ever could. I'm cleaning up his mess, like I always do. And you know what? I *am* going to have his bank access shut down. See how well he does without someone else's work supporting him."

At some point, she'd stood up, and now paced in the short space around the bed, West's brows practically gone beneath the brim of his usual navy cap.

"Well, you know, maybe." He waved a hand, then stood

up. "Let's just take a breath. Sit down. You don't have to respond this minute."

"Yes, I do. I have to send that email to my investigator so he can do whatever computer magic he does to trace it. Then go find him, and…and…"

"And what?"

"I don't know!" She grunted and then flung her arms toward the ceiling before flopping her bum back onto the bed.

West didn't sit beside her. He also didn't let her reach for the laptop again, snagging her hands as she leaned and pulling them in front of himself as he squatted down to be more on eye level with her again.

"We made him angry, and now he's lashing out. We made him angry so he'd talk, right?"

"It's one thing to say those things to me. It's another to say those things to you, and the implication that you were lowering yourself."

"That must have been one of the Portuguese bits."

"Yep," she confirmed, then decided against translating anything else. "He didn't have to say those things to you."

"No, he didn't. And you're right to be angry, but if you respond to him angrily, there is no way to salvage this." His voice was gentle, and when she looked at his hands again, her ring was back on his finger, where it had been yesterday when he wasn't on duty. "An angry email is worse than no email at all. Send it to your investigator, and let it sit until you don't want to break his heart in return."

She wiggled one of her hands free so she could trace it around the ring. It worked; she'd asked him to break her father's silence, and he'd done it.

"Forward it to me, and I'll forward to my investigator. Though I don't really know what I want him to do. Aside from go there and slap some sense into him."

A couple of minutes later that had been sorted, but she still wanted to send him an email in all caps.

"Before this morning, what was it you wanted to happen with him? You said you wanted him to know everything was okay, and have his health checked, right? Did you see him having any part of the business in the future?"

"Yes, just not the work."

"The pomp and ceremonies?" he asked.

She nodded.

"You can still have that. You're not converting to a distillery. There is no MacIntyre Whiskey. Right?"

Again, she nodded. This time, he lifted her hands as he straightened from his squat, pulling her to her feet and directly into a tight hug.

"Remember, he isn't himself. He might have been drunk when he emailed. He might be affected by his hypothyroidism. And he knows right where to hit you to make it hurt the most."

His words were nice, but the fact that he'd done anything at all was nicer. And nicest of all was the warm arms around her, and the heart thudding beneath her cheek. "This is what I need, you know?"

To make sure he didn't misunderstand, she squeezed him tight.

"Me, too," came the soft reply, and a nuzzle in her hair.

"I want my ring back."

He laughed at her grumpy demand, and although she was admittedly sulking and probably pouting, and definitely mentally picturing all the ways she wanted to scream at her father, West took the grumpy demand, let go of her and sunk right down to one knee.

She pushed the hood down on her fuzzy pink onesie, and splayed the fingers of her right hand expectantly, a smile starting to come back to her face as he twisted and tugged on the ring. "Are you going to say new words this time?"

"I might need to ask you to go get some of the ultrasound jelly…"

"It's stuck?"

He licked his finger, gave another twisting yank and the intricate band finally slipped past his knuckle. "Sorry, it's a little slobbered on."

She wiggled her finger, anyway, laughing. "And many years from now, when our children ask to hear the story of how Pai proposed, we'll sigh wistfully and say, 'Sorry, it's a little slobbered on.'"

"No, we've got time to come up with a better story than that." He slipped it onto her finger, and it settled into the well-worn rut that had not yet filled back in. Comfortably back where it was supposed to have been. "Maybe something like this beautiful ring that we designed together represents the wonderful life and family we will build together."

Words she'd painfully lobbed at him when she'd first arrived, but twisted to add new promises where promises had been broken.

She couldn't think of anything to add, just shook her hands at him urgently until he stood up, and she launched herself at him, her arms flinging around his shoulders as she kissed the side of his neck and said one word, "Bed."

"I thought you were supposed to say *yes*. Last time you said *yes*." He chuckled at her, back to teasing as his arms wrapped eagerly around her.

"Yes," she said, then, *"Sim."* And, while backing toward the bed, "Bed—*cama*."

He didn't let go, the biggest smile on his face as they waddle-swayed back toward the thing. "We only have—" he paused to check the clock "—fifteen minutes before shift starts."

"We can do a lot in fifteen minutes." She let go of him just long enough to yank down the zipper on her onesie while his lips found her and he fumbled for his trousers.

EPILOGUE

One week later...

WEST STOOD WITH Lia and all nonessential personnel in the lounge, lights off, before a long bank of windows showing a midnight-dark late-afternoon sky.

"I've got another ten minutes before my window closes, have a call at seven I need to prepare for," the captain said, casting a dubious eye toward the windows and the sky utterly devoid of aurora.

"If they don't come, we'll do it tomorrow," West said, standing behind her, his arms wrapped around her heavily insulated body. Her wedding outfit was standard-issue red, and they were planning to make a mad dash out into the howling wind to say, "I do," and kiss, just as soon as the first shock of color arrived.

She shook her head, and argued, "They'll come. I have a good feeling."

Everything else had come together, from the captain agreeing to the odd wedding, to the galley cooks baking a cake, to Eileen lending her metalsmithing skills to smelt and polish some tinfoil from a ripped out, unused section of ventilation to make West a proper, non-silicone-gasket ring.

The only thing that was missing was an internet connection, so Jordan and Zeke could witness from their sunny,

Southern California beach. But she was recording it to upload once the satellite passed over.

Just after the captain had given the five-minute warning, the sky began to glow ever so faintly blue.

Someone shouted it out, and a stampede of red suits made for the nearest exit, funneling through. The sky was clear—it had to be to see them—but wind was an issue today. A blast smashed her into West as she turned to face him, and with them both grinning and gripping cold, gloveless hands, the captain began talking. Not that they could hear anything. They got their cues by him slapping one of them on the arm and making gestures and mouthing, "Do you?" at each in turn, and pausing for a nod. Finally, he jabbed a gloved finger at their hands, and they hurriedly crammed rings onto stiff unruly fingers as the sky finally lit up. A wave of blue undulating to purple and pink rippled past them, and while she still had her eyes toward the heavens, West grabbed her by the cheeks and got his kiss.

Three minutes flat, probably the fastest wedding in Antarctic history, and they all ran back inside, teeth chattering but big smiles. On their way to the cake, which was probably why everyone showed up, the guests formed lines from the door to the lounge, inside, and tossed homemade construction paper confetti at them—because no one was willing to waste dry-goods staples at the start of winter, but everyone wanted cake.

Much later, after they'd adjourned to the sauna to thaw out a little, and did their best to steam up the bubble window on the cabin they now shared, Lia lay with her cheek on his chest, her favorite position, and they watched the window, which had now gone dark and starry again.

"Aurora." She said the first name that came to her mind of all the things she wanted to plan for.

"Where?"

"If we have a daughter her name should be Aurora."

"And if it's a boy?"

She squeezed his waist with the arm she always draped over it, then whispered, "Charlie."

His chest dipped in sudden and quick, bouncing her head slightly as he felt for her hand, and squeezed. He didn't say anything—he didn't need to. She slid up to him, and hugged his head, pressing her cheek to his for as long as he needed it, and that was progress.

Just as she was giving up to comfort and exhaustion, she heard him whisper, *"Amo-te."*

And she whispered back, "Always."

* * * * *

LET'S TALK
Romance

For exclusive extracts, competitions
and special offers, find us online:

- facebook.com/millsandboon
- @millsandboonuk
- @millsandboon

Or get in touch on 0844 844 1351*

For all the latest titles coming soon,
visit millsandboon.co.uk/nextmonth

*Calls cost 7p per minute plus your phone company's price per
minute access charge